Mittens

In The

Boundary

Waters

Mittens In The Boundary Waters
By
Larry Ahlman

International Standard Book No. 0-9712906-0-1

Mittens in the boundary waters / by Larry Ahlman

Published by Kodiak Publishing Co.
9525 W. 230 St.
Morristown, MN 55052
(507) 685-4246
www.ahlmans.com

Wolf sketch on page 137: Brandon Lutterman
All other illustrations & Cover painting: Dana Hanson
Prints of Dana Hanson artwork available from:
Lord Warmington Studio
PO Box 1088
Faribault, MN 55021
(507) 332-6756
www.Lordwarmingtonstudio.com

Editor: Chuck Larson

Copy production: Kay Richey
KLR Communications, Inc.
6767 Miller Rd.
Buckley, MI 49620
(231) 263-7381 Fax (231) 263-7898

Printed by Modern Printers
Faribault, MN 55021
(507) 334-2275
www.modernprinters.com

0 9 7 1 2 9 0 6 0 1

Dedication

To my good friend, Jerry Schaefer, whose boundless enthusiasm for life occasionally rubs off on people like me, causing them to swim oceans, move mountains, soar with eagles or . . .write a book.

Foreword

By

Larry Ahlman

The early 1930s were desperate times in America. As the country struggled through the Great Depression, many of its finest young men — unable to find work — turned to begging or stealing to get by. And many began roaming the country, searching for their dream.

Many stories are told about the plight of these young men, but none touched me as deeply as the story of Charles "Mittens" Perkins, who traveled to the Boundary Waters Wilderness of Northern Minnesota in 1931 — searching for his dream.

Intrigued by the story, I attempted to document it but could find no written record. In a further effort, I hiked to the area in the story, searching for traces of his cabin and the mystical twin falls of the Ahmoo, but found neither.

Then again, few records were kept during the depression years, especially for people of lesser means. Wilderness cabins — built on wet ground — tend to rot away quickly. And the Ahmoo Creek, with its rugged terrain and difficult to follow tributaries, could hide many secrets.

So, is the story true? Well...you be the judge.

Contents

Chapter 1

Hardware Hardship

While balancing a crate of lantern globes on his shoulder, Mittens placed two wooden beverage containers on end and gingerly climbed on top of them. When he stretched his arms, trying to place the crate on the top shelf, the teetering containers suddenly tipped sideways. As he let go of the crate, it crashed to the floor while he jumped to safety.

"You stupid idiot," yelled Fred, the gray haired owner of the hardware store where Mittens worked. "You were born with feet where your hands should be and brains in your butt. I've seen clumsy people before, but you're the worst."

"Hey! I landed on my feet and didn't get hurt. Did you expect me to risk my neck over a lousy crate of lantern globes?"

"Lousy? Just wait until I take them out of your wages. Then I'll see if you still call them lousy. Now, get out of here and go home. I don't want to look at your stupid face any more today."

"Stupid face?" he muttered, as he walked out the door. "The only thing stupid is Fred's attitude. He doesn't have an ounce of respect for what I do and he never will."

Respect was an elusive goal in the small town of Hibbing, Minnesota in 1931 and Mittens was having a hard time finding it. The victim of a broken family, he had left St. Paul a few years earlier to look for work in the iron mines. After dropping a box of explosives, almost causing a catastrophe, he was fired. When the news got around, he couldn't find a mine in the region that would hire him. But he liked the North Country and remained in his rented apartment — a few blocks from downtown — and did menial jobs wherever he could find work. Lacking a car, he felt that walking to work was just fine.

His real name was Charles Perkins, but everybody called him "Mittens" because of his fondness for big gloves. Since freezing his hands as a child, his fingers were sensitive to cold and he kept them bundled nine months out of the year. In winter, he wore big fur mittens that came halfway to his elbows and he'd bare his hands only in the heat of summer.

He was a big man — over 6 feet tall and crowding 300 pounds — but he intimidated no one. With puffy red cheeks and a baby face, this 21 year old looked like he was still in his early teens. He wasn't overly bright and a bit on the clumsy side, but he had a heart of gold. But a heart of gold wouldn't get you by in this rugged iron range town. You needed money and respect and he had neither.

Walking home, he crossed the railroad tracks that he'd crossed so many times before. The tracks came out of the Hibbing rail yard, crossed the highway and disappeared into the woods. Stopping to rest, he sat on a nearby fence, looked longingly at the tracks and wondered why they intrigued him. Perhaps it was the mystery of where they went as they disappeared into the woods. He often wondered, "Do those tracks lead to some magical place?"

Often he wished he could just leave, head down those tracks and see what marvelous things he'd find. Perhaps he'd find a mystical place where the deer roam, the birds sing and all the people are nice. Maybe he'd find a place of solitude among the pines, build a log house and live there. But his wandering spirit was tempered by the hard reality of life: the country was reeling in the depths of depression, jobs and money were hard to come by and he felt fortunate just to have a roof over his head and food on the table.

As he continued down the road, he arrived at the old house with gray slab siding that he called home.

13

An elderly lady, Mary Larsen, owned the house and rented the upstairs apartment to him. She was a good person, always kind to him and she'd often let the rent slide or have him do repairs to the house when he was short of money. Her late husband left her a pile of guns and fishing tackle and she let Mittens use them whenever he wanted, which was often.

He had a knack for shooting, but a hard time outwitting game. He was also unlucky at fishing. But every once in awhile he'd bag a couple rabbits or catch a few fish. When he did, he'd proudly hand them to Mrs. Larsen, who was a great cook and part of the reason why he was overweight. She didn't mind cleaning and cooking fish or birds, but she had a hang-up with rabbits and usually scolded Mittens while she was cutting them up. "How can you shoot something that's this cute?" "Hey! I'm a hunter," he'd reply, "and that's food."

Climbing the long set of stairs that led to his apartment, he could hear familiar barking. It was his dog Millie who was always anxious to greet him. Millie was part border collie and part terrier with a pinch of labrador thrown in. He found her a few years ago — abandoned as a pup. The previous owner apparently didn't want a mixed breed dog and dumped her. Mittens didn't want her either, but when she looked up at him with her soft brown eyes, he melted and took her home.

As he opened the door, she leaped up and licked his face. "Well, old girl, you've been cooped up all day long. Let's go outside." Soon they were on the lawn, doing their daily routine. Millie, with her little bit of labrador blood, loved to retrieve and each day Mittens spent a half hour tossing an old ragged baseball across the lawn for her to fetch. Playing ball with Millie, along with his hunting and fishing, kept his mind off the hard scrabble life he led and the indignity of Fred and the hardware store.

BACK TO THE SALT MINES

The next morning he said his usual good-bye to the dog and headed for work. When he arrived at the hardware store, Fred was in another bad mood. "Take this box of nails over to the Carrigan place. They need them right away."

"That's a mile and a half walk," said Mittens. "It'll take me most of the morning."

"Then you'd better get going instead of standing around here."

Grabbing the 50 pound box of nails, he headed out the door. After walking a few blocks, lugging the heavy load, he spotted a Model A pulling a big hay trailer. "If I wait until he goes by," he thought, "I can hitch a ride on the back and he won't see me."

As the trailer passed, he stepped behind it, tossed the box of nails on and jumped aboard. Bouncing along on the bumpy road, he laid back on the pile of hay and watched the clouds pass by. When he arrived at the Carrigan place, he grabbed the box of nails and jumped off. To his shock, the box was empty. He had placed it

15

on the wagon upside down and the cover slid off, slowly spilling the contents onto the road.

Tossing the empty box in the ditch, he thought, "I'm in trouble now," and started walking back to the hardware store. After walking a block, he spotted a car pulled over to the side with the driver fixing a flat tire. A block later, two more cars were sitting by the side of the road with flat tires. By the time he reached downtown, he had lost count of all the disabled vehicles.

The problem had turned into more than a lost box of nails: he was in a lot of trouble. Pausing outside the hardware store, he weighed his options: If he told the truth, he'd likely be fired. And, even if he wasn't fired, when word got around who the culprit was that spread nails on the road, everyone in town would be after him to pay for their tires. He decided to take care of the situation his own way.

Opening the door, he barely stepped inside when Fred started yelling again. "About time you got back. Get on over to Scotts. That pump you put in for them still overheats."

"Then go fix it yourself," said Mittens. "I'm not taking anymore guff from you."

"You'd better watch that tongue of yours, Sonny. Don't forget, I was nice enough to give you a job when no one else in town would hire you."

"Well, you can take your nice little job and your crummy old store and stick it where the sun doesn't

16

shine. I'm leaving!"

"Oh yah! Just try to find someplace else. Go ahead, see if anyone will hire a low life bum like you. And when you're done looking, come back and apologize to me and maybe I'll let you have your job back."

"Yah! I think I'll do that," replied Mittens. "And I think you ought to fix your front door. It closes kind of hard." As he walked out, he slammed the door so hard it almost came off the hinges. "That felt good," he chuckled.

Millie happily wagged her tail to see her master home early. "We've got a little problem, girl. I might be going away for awhile. Let's take a walk."

When he returned, a police car was parked in front of the house and the officer was talking to Mrs. Larsen. Grabbing Millie, he stepped behind a clump of trees and waited. When the police left, Mittens returned and started up the stairs.

Mrs. Larsen yelled up, "Are you in some kind of trouble?"

"No, just a little misunderstanding. I'll have it all straightened out in the morning."

That night, he kept the lights off and sat by the window, watching to see if the police would return. "I hate this apartment," he groaned. " I hate this town and I hate my job. That is, if I even have a job anymore. Who knows! At the rate I'm going, I might end up in chains — busting rocks for the county. But that would

17

be better than working for old Fred."

That night, between fits of sleeplessness, he had a dream. He dreamed he was roaming the country, free of responsibility and free to do whatever he pleased with no one to tell him what to do. The urge to roam had turned into an obsession he could no longer deny. As the first light of dawn brightened his room, he made a decision to unshackle his free spirit. He was leaving town.

He was nearly broke, but with his youth, health and a half-breed dog, what more could he wish for? With this newly found feeling of freedom, he started to pack. "I'm going on a trip and you're coming along," he said to Millie.

Rummaging through the apartment, he grabbed everything of value and laid it on the table. After looking over the three year accumulation, he had a tough time seeing any value at all and decided to leave most of it behind. Sorting through the pile one more time, he crammed the remainder into one large suitcase. After writing Mrs. Larsen a note, telling her she could keep everything that was left, he walked out the door.

Sticking close to the trees in case the police returned, he hiked to the railroad tracks and sat on his familiar perch on the fence. "We're through looking at these tracks and wondering where they go," he said to Millie. "Today, we're going to find out." Grabbing the suitcase, he started down the tracks and didn't look back. Soon, the jackpines along the sides of the tracks caused

18

the scenery to look like a long deep canyon. He had broken the bonds of conformity that tried to rule his life and for the first time, felt free.

Chapter 2

The Taste Of Freedom

Energized with his new found freedom, Mittens walked briskly. He felt unburdoned. He felt free. His suitcase, however, felt like it was full of lead, so he stopped to lighten it. First, he removed all the pictures from the frames, folded them in a neat bundle and threw away the heavy frames. Then he started throwing clothes, extra shoes, tools, books and Millie's ball. As the ball bounced against the track and rolled off the steep grade of the railroad bed, she ran after it. When she brought it back, Mittens stuck it back in the suitcase. "I guess we have to draw the line somewhere," he said.

As the miles wore on, the suitcase was still a burden. Opening it up, he sifted through the contents and carefully selected only his most treasured items.

Tearing off a leg from a pair of trousers, he knotted the end and made a small packsack. After stuffing the last of his worldly belongings into the pack. He put the rest inside the suitcase and hid it near a large pine tree. He still had a nagging feeling that this urge to roam would subside. When it did, he'd turn around, retrieve the suitcase and head back to Hibbing to face his problems.

With the lighter pack sack, the skip in his step returned and he often started singing to the rhythm of his steps. As he walked the tracks to no place in particular with a pack bouncing on his back, it occurred to him that he was becoming what some folks refer to as a "Vagabond" or "Hobo". But he didn't mind. Maybe he was poor, but he was young and free. He didn't care what tomorrow would bring. Right now, the world was his.

The tracks dragged on in an endless ribbon. Each time they'd curve, he expected to see a new and wondrous sight around the bend. But when the curve straightened, the monotonous tree lined tunnel continued. Finally it passed through an open meadow and he stopped to rest. Millie spotted something in the middle of the meadow and went charging after it. Suddenly Mittens spotted the small black object she was heading for. It was a skunk.

After whistling loudly, he yelled, "Come back!" But she wouldn't listen and ran up to see what kind of creature this was. As she approached the skunk, its back hunched high and the beady little eyes glared at the dog. Wagging her tail in friendship, Millie walked closer. When she was 5 feet away, the skunk spun around, lifted its tail and gave her a blast in the face. Letting out a yelp, she ran away, stopping every ten feet to push her face through the grass. "Maybe next time you'll listen when I tell you to stop," said Mittens as they climbed back on the rail bed.

Continuing on, they arrived at a bridge that crossed a small creek. While Millie rolled around in the water, trying to rid herself of the smell, Mittens pulled his boots off, sat on a rock by the creek and cooled his feet in the chilly water. He wasn't accustomed to missing his noon meal and after all the walking, he was starting to get hungry. "When you see pictures of hobos in a magazine, they always look ragged and dirty," he mused. "But they also look fat. I wonder what they eat?"

After following the tracks a few more miles, he arrived in the small town of Virginia. The train yard was bustling with activity. Locomotives, flatcars, boxcars and scores of mining cars were clanging and banging as the workers shuffled and re-arranged them. There were so many tracks that he couldn't figure out which ones went where. Suddenly someone yelled at him from a nearby boxcar. As he glanced at the car, a hand stuck out of the doorway, motioning him to come over.

As he approached, a grubby looking fellow poked his head out and said, "Jump in. No sense in walking when you can ride."

"Where's it going"? yelled Mittens.

"This one's heading south for Duluth. That's where all the action is. Better get in before she starts rolling."

Picking up Millie, he tossed her into the boxcar and jumped aboard.

"Holy Cow! That dog smells like a skunk," yelled the hobo. "Get her off."

"No way!" yelled Mittens. "Where I go, the dog goes."

"OK, but tie her up at the far end of the car."

After tying Millie, he took a look at the gloomy surroundings. The wood walls of the boxcar were dark with filth and the floor was covered with 3 inches of old dung. Among its many uses, the car had been used for hauling livestock. The dung was slick and slippery and the smell was certainly worse than Millie.

As he moved away from the lighted doorway towards a darkened corner, he could see the faces of several other derelicts who were lined against the walls, sitting on sheets of cardboard. With their ragged clothes and unshaven faces, they were a sorry looking bunch. As he stood there in his clean white shirt and pressed trousers, they stared coldly at him as if they were jackals — ready to have him for lunch. Deciding that this boxcar wasn't the safest place for him to be, he made a quick decision to leave.

As he walked to the other end of the car to untie Millie, he heard a distant clunk, clunk, clunk grow louder as the cars took up the slack. As the boxcar suddenly lurched forward, Mittens lost his balance and sprawled head first into the livestock dung. As he got back on his feet, he looked at his shirt. It was smeared brown and when he turned around, several of the vagrants were laughing at him.

He tried to get off the train, but by the time he untied the dog and got back to the door, the scenery was whizzing by; it was too late. He was stuck on the train with this unruly group. The vagrants continued laughing and one yelled, "Hey fatso! Where can I get one of those white shirts with the brown stripes?" The rest of them laughed heartily.

His anger began to grow. He had left Hibbing to get away from people who laughed and made jokes of him. Except for Mrs. Larsen, no one in town respected him. Now in the company of hobos, the scum of the earth, even they were treating him like he was a second class citizen. As the laughter continued, his temper flared and he stared coldly at the group. Then a strange thing happened: As the laughter continued, it became contagious. Mittens looked at his shirt and started laughing along with them.

He wasn't second class after all. He was one of them, and soon he was shaking hands and introducing himself. There were about a dozen men in the car. Most were in their twenties and all of them were down on their luck. With his clean clothes and shaved face, he still felt out of place among this group. But they were all in the same boat he was and they all laughed when he told his story about the box of nails.

Mittens was sensitive to bad smells and with the temperature closing in on 90, the manure in the car was giving off a pungent odor that was annoying him. Looking for fresh air, he walked over to the door, sat down and hung his feet outside. As the train continued south, he watched the green blur of the pine trees whisking by and joked, "I wonder what kind of trouble I can get into in Duluth? I'll find out pretty soon, I guess."

Soon the cars started banging like a row of falling dominoes as the train began to slow for a sharp curve. A short time later it turned again. Now they were heading north. Turning to one of the vagrants, Mittens asked, "You sure this manure bucket is going to Duluth?"

"Maybe I screwed up. This could be the train to Tower. But no problem. If it is, you can just switch to the next one going south."

By now it had been a long time since he ate. He was hungry and was learning that life as a hobo includes long stretches between meals. One of the fellows had a big hunk of cheese in his pocket which he passed around. When it came to Mittens, he took a close look and decided he'd have to be a lot hungrier before he ate something like that.

The train slowed to a snails pace as it continued

north. The expanse of trees and swamps seemed endless with only a rare glimpse of civilization. Finally they arrived in Tower. As they entered the train yard, the hobos started jumping off while the train was still moving.

"What's the hurry," yelled Mittens.

"They've got a tough yardmaster here," one of them yelled. "A retired cop named Joe. You'd better hightail it because he doesn't take kindly to train jumpers."

He decided to wait until the train stopped — a big mistake. As he was climbing out of the boxcar, a fellow with a two foot long policemans night stick spotted him. It was Joe. Mittens took off running with the fellow in hot pursuit. Millie, seeing her master in trouble, turned on the pursuer and sunk her teeth into his leg. With a swift blow from the night stick, Joe smacked Millie in the mid-section and sent her sprawling onto the tracks.

As he walked up to the dog to deliver another blow, Mittens let out a holler and raced towards him. Joe assumed a baseball stance and as Mittens lunged at him, he stepped to the side and cracked him in the ribs with the nightstick. Mittens outweighed him two to one, but the old cop was quicker. As he lunged again, Joe busted him behind the knee with the night stick and sent him sprawling to the ground. Before he could get up, Joe was wailing the tar out of him with the stick and all Mittens could think about was protecting his head from the blows.

Suddenly Joe let out a yell. Millie was chewing on his ankle again. Seeing his chance, Mittens grabbed the other leg, gave it a yank, and Joe went down. Mittens picked up the nightstick and started returning the punishment. Suddenly he heard yelling. Two other railroad workers were running towards him.

Grabbing Millie by the collar, he charged into the nearby trees and didn't slow down until he was deep in the woods. Finally he stopped and plunked himself down on a log to check his wounds. He had welts all over his arms and back and his knee was starting to stiffen. But he'd get over it. And, he had a nice souvenir of the experience: a policemans nightstick. Playfully slapping Millie on the rump with the stick, he said, "When are you going to start listening to me when I yell?"

Darkness was closing in and he decided to "rough it" and spend the night in the woods. Taking out his pocket knife, he cut several pine boughs to make a bed and got a fire going. With the temperature that high, he didn't need heat, but the smoke helped keep the mosquitoes away. "Now if I can find something to eat, I'll be in good shape," he thought.

Digging through his makeshift pack, he found a couple sticks of jerky and a few pieces of candy; not enough to make a meal. Tossing one to Millie, he said, "We'll find more in the morning."

Laying down on the pine boughs, he thought about the events of the day. He had only left Hibbing that morning, yet so much had happened during the day that he felt like a week had passed. He hadn't planned on this much excitement, but it sure beat the boredom of working in the hardware store.

The next morning he headed back to Tower and paused before entering town. Getting to Duluth meant going to the rail yard, hopping a southbound train and hoping Joe and his bunch of cronies wouldn't catch him. With his sore knee and aching ribs reminding him how unfriendly those railroad folks are, he decided to put the trip off for a day. Staying in the safety of the woods, he hiked east until he had passed the town, then jumped back on the tracks. "Let me see. I can't go back to Hibbing and I can't go back to Tower," he mused. "At the rate I'm burning bridges behind me, pretty soon there'll be no place left to go."

A mile out of Tower, he spotted a small country homestead with a barn and milk cows. With his stomach growling from lack of food, he decided to stop and ask if he could buy something to eat. Feeling like a beggar, he knocked on the door. A crusty old man named Gus Schilling opened the door and said, "What do you want?"

"I haven't eaten for a while. Can I buy some food? I've got money."

Pointing west, he said, "If you got money, go back to Tower. They sell food there."

Mittens explained his problem with the railroad

people and why he didn't feel comfortable hanging around town.

"OK, I guess I can help you out," Gus chuckled. "I never cared much for them railroad people myself. They think they own everything. I'll tell you what I'll do. If you'll cut down that dead tree over there, saw it up and pile the firewood by the house, I'll have the wife cook you a meal."

"That's the best offer I've had today, I'll do it."

By mid day, he had the wood pile half built. Suddenly the house door swung open and Gus yelled, "Soups on." His wife was a good cook and after dinner, Mittens offered to finish off the wood pile if he could spend the night in the barn and get breakfast in the morning. They took him up on the offer.

Following breakfast, he stayed around and talked to Gus for a long time, telling him his life history and explaining how the mines had his number and wouldn't hire him. He wanted to stay around the area, but couldn't find work that he liked. When he mentioned how he enjoyed being out in the woods, Gus said, "Have you ever tried trapping? Those trappers make a ton of money. They've got lots of freedom and don't have to answer to anyone."

"Maybe so," said Mittens. "But I don't know a thing about trapping. I doubt if I could catch anything. And it takes lots of money to buy the equipment. I couldn't buy ten traps with what I've got."

"I'll tell you what to do. Head over to Winton and look up a fellow named Jack Denley.

Tell him I sent you. I heard that his partner pulled out and he needs help. If he likes you, he might hire you and teach you how to run a line. It's worth a try."

Chapter 3

Meeting Old Jack

After thanking Gus, he decided to forget about Duluth for now and walk to Winton to talk to the old trapper. After many hours of walking, he reached the town of Ely and soon the town of Winton appeared. Winton was the end of the line for the railroad and the end of the line for almost everything else. Beyond the town was a vast wilderness that stretched east to Lake Superior and deep into Canada. Some called it the Roadless Area and others called it the Boundary Waters. Trains or cars were useless in that place and the only practical way to get around was by canoe in the summer and dog team in the winter.

Leaving the train yard, he walked into town and paused on the main street. It looked like this remnant of the big pine logging era was nearly deserted. Since the closing of the big mill, most of the people had left and a lot of the buildings were run down and crumbling from neglect. To add more dreariness to the town, it started to rain.

As the unpaved streets turned muddy, his boots turned into big balls of mud as he slogged through the middle of town and tried to find a dry place to walk. Spotting a cafe, he decided to stop and ask for directions to Jack's place. After scraping several pounds of mud off his boots, he tied Millie to a post and pushed open the door, causing a small bell to jingle — announcing his arrival.

The tables were empty except for two elderly gentlemen who were playing cards and drinking coffee. After getting directions from them, and heading for the door, his sensitive nose detected a fragrance so wonderful that it made him stop: freshly baked blueberry pie. Unable to resist its appeal, he headed for the counter and plunked himself down on one of the round stools.

A minute later, a girl in her early twenties walked out of the kitchen and over to the counter. Not just any girl, but a girl of such striking beauty that the whole room seemed to brighten as she entered. As he glanced at her sweet smile and flowing brown hair, it made him wonder why some city slicker from St. Paul hadn't rescued this "Belle of the North" from her fate in this frontier town. With a voice so sweet it sounded like music, she said, "Hi! I'm Louise. Can I get you something?"

"Um...Ah...Yes! I smell blueberry pie. Can I get a piece of it?"

"You sure can. I just took it out of the oven. I'll be right back."

His heart was fluttering as he watched her walk back to the kitchen, but he knew better than to get his hopes up. After all, one lesson he learned in Hibbing was that pretty girls don't go for 300 pound guys. And, they don't go for fellows who wear old clothes, don't have a car and are eternally short of cash. As hard as he tried, he could never get a date. Even the homely girls turned him down.

When Louise returned with the pie, it was still steaming as she placed it in front of him. As he quickly gulped it down, she asked if he wanted another piece.

"I'd love to have more," he replied. "But I'm sort of on a budget for awhile."

"Oh that's no problem. The next one's free. I don't get that many customers for pie."

As he consumed the second piece, she said," Excuse me for asking, but how did you get those strange brown streaks on your white shirt?"

Slightly embarrassed, he replied, "Well, it's kind of a long story and I'm sure you don't want to hear it."

"Yes, I do. Tell me."

As he slowly rattled off his tale about terror on the train and his slide onto the messy manure floor, she started to laugh. Not an insulting laugh like he was used to hearing, but a sweet and friendly laugh that made him feel at ease. This girl was really special.

"I can imagine how much fun it would be to ride in a boxcar," she said. "But I'd be afraid of getting caught. Those railroad people are rough on trespassers. A bunch of rail workers stop here every Tuesday for lunch and they often brag about how they just beat up some train jumper."

"Did you ever run across a railroad worker named Joe?" said Mittens.

"You must mean Old Joe from Tower. He's the worst one of the bunch. I hate it when that guy comes in, cussing and twirling his nightstick. He's a jerk and I can't stand him."

A big smile appeared on his face as he told her of how he and Millie got the best of Old Joe in the scuffle they had over in Tower.

"I don't believe it," she said. "You're just joking. Right?"

His smile turned into a broad grin as he reached down, unhooked Joe's nightstick from his belt and laid it on the counter.

"Then it's really true," she said. "Old Joe finally met his match. This is great. Can I meet this brave dog that you have?"

"Sure. She's right outside the door."

After they stepped outside, she leaned down and gave the dog a big hug. "You're such a nice dog and you have such beautiful brown eyes," she said. Millie responded by splashing Louise's face with her long tongue.

"Will you be in town very long?" she said.

"Just for a couple days, I guess."

"Well, maybe you could stop back and see me. I'll have Mom watch the cafe and we'll go for a walk by the lake."

"Maybe?" thought Mittens. There would be no "Maybe" about it.

"That would be fun." he said. "I'll be back soon. Real soon."

As he walked away, he was floating on a cloud. This girl was one in a million and seemed to genuinely like him — the kind of girl he had pictured in his dreams. A girl he would love to whisk away to his mystical cabin in the woods where he would spend the rest of his life treating her like a queen and working hard to make her happy.

But then he thought, "It can never be. She's too pretty to fall for somebody like me. She's lonely because there's not many young fellows in town and she'd probably cheat on me the first chance she got. She thinks I'm a hero for getting the best of Old Joe, but I left out a couple key parts of the story: I was running away when the scuffle started and I was running away when it ended. Eventually, she'll find out I'm not a hero and it will be over. No, rather than let her break my heart, I think I'll just end things right now. Well...maybe."

Continuing through the mud, he walked down to the lake to look for Jack's place. When he found it, he shook his head in disgust; junk was heaped in piles so high that it touched the rusted steel roofs of the crumbling buildings. The place was so messy that it made the muddy streets of the town look good.

As he approached the gate on the big fence that secured the place, a dozen or more sled dogs spotted him and Millie. As the dogs tore up to the gate, snarling and barking, he was thankful that the fence was well built. Suddenly a voice from one of the buildings shouted, "Shut Up!" and the dogs dutifully returned to their quarters.

Emerging from one of the buildings was a tall skinny fellow with a long gray beard and deerskin clothing that looked like it hadn't seen soap and water for years. His deep piercing eyes and the wild look on his face made you want to reach down to see if your wallet was still there. Mittens said, "Are you Jack Denley?"

"Yah, that's me. What do you want?"

"Gus Schilling sent me. He said you might need some help."

"I need a trapper, and you don't look like a trapper to me."

"Maybe not," said Mittens. "But I'm a hard worker. I learn fast and I'll make you a lot of money."

"Sure you will. A greenhorn like you will just get lost out there and I'll be spending all my time finding you. Beat it kid. You're no trapper and I got work to do."

Mittens was a slow thinker and when insulted, it took him a long time to respond. The insulting rejection by Jack demanded response, but unable to find the right words, he turned and started slowly sulking back up the hill. Suddenly he stopped, turned around and bellowed, "You old Coot! You're no trapper either. I'll bet you can't even catch a cold."

Chuckling at the absurd challenge, Jack opened the gate and said, "Come on back and we'll talk a bit. But leave that mongrel of yours tied outside or my dogs will have her for lunch."

Following Jack, he tiptoed past the growling dogs, then ducking his head and pulling in his stomach, squeezed through the tiny doorway of the dilapidated building that Jack called home. The house reeked with the smell of animal hides and trapping lures which caused Mittens to wonder if this is really the business he wanted to be in.

Motioning for him to sit in the chair next to the kitchen table, Jack poured a couple cups of a vile brew that resembled coffee and said, "So you want me to teach you how to trap and then turn you loose in the woods. What makes you think you can handle it?"

"I've had a dream for years. I've dreamed of getting away from people. I've dreamed of building a cabin in the wilderness, far from everything. I've spent a few nights in the woods and I feel comfortable there. If you won't work with me, I'll find someone else. Or I'll just do it on my own."

"That's a real touching speech," said Jack. "You don't know what you're getting into. But I need to find someone pretty soon and I guess you're the one. I'll spend a few days teaching you the trade and if you catch on fast, we'll work out some kind of deal."

"That's great! You won't regret it."

"Of course, while you're here, I'll expect you to feed the dogs, do the cooking and a few other chores to earn your keep. You can sleep over there in that corner."

Eyeing the pile of rags and smelly hides in the corner, Mittens replied, "Thanks! But if you don't mind, I'll stay with my dog in that grove of trees outside the fence."

The next morning, he tied Millie to a tree outside the fence and quietly opened the big iron gate. He was only halfway through when the dogs started growling. Reaching in his pocket, he pulled out a handful of hard rock candy and started throwing pieces of it at the dogs. While they chased around for the candy, he slowly sneaked over to the house.

Jack was still in bed, snoring like an old horse, as Mittens fired up the big cast iron cookstove and started frying pancakes. As the heat of the stove amplified the smell of the hides and lures, he noticed another new smell: Jack, apparently suffering from intestinal problems, was passing profuse quantities of gas. As the room got hotter, the various odors blended together and began to overwhelm Mittens. It was worse than the livestock car he had ridden in.

He soon figured out a way to neutralize the odors. Cranking up the fire in the stove, he burned the pancakes until they were reduced to small black cinders that were sending up plumes of smoke. Smelling the smoke, Jack woke up, put on his boots, splashed his face with water and sat down at the table. The blackened pancakes were rock hard and made a clanking sound as Mittens dropped them onto Jack's plate. "Not bad," he said as he dug into them. "At least you know how to cook."

After breakfast, Jack introduced him to the dogs while Millie paced nervously outside the fence. "These guys are a bit on the wild side, but if you keep reminding them who the boss is, you'll get along fine. You won't be taking a team out, but you may have to handle them on the way back in. By the way, you're not thinking about taking your mongrel along on the trapline?"

"Where I go, Millie goes," said Mittens.

"That's up to you. But I'll give that dog a week,

maybe two before the wolves make a meal out of her."

"I'm not afraid of them. If a wolf messes around with us, I'll blow it away."

Over the next several days, Jack showed him how to build trapping sets, how to skin and stretch hides and how to live off the land. Between the training sessions and all the chores, Jack kept him so busy that he never found the time to go into town and visit Louise. And as he slowly convinced himself that she probably wasn't the right girl for him anyway, he began to feel that it was best to try to forget her.

Finally Jack laid out his plan: "East of here is the Roadless Area," he said as he pulled out a big map and spread it on the table. Pointing to a place called Insula Lake, he said, "I've got trapping permits in this area. One to the north near Ima Lake and another south of Insula between Wilder and Arrow Lake. My partner pulled out this spring and I need someone to set up and work a line in the south area while I do the north. He left all his traps and gear with me and I can outfit you with everything you need."

"And what's in it for me?"

"When we sell the pelts, you keep half of what you catch, less any equipment you lose."

"And what about your furs," said Mittens. "It sounds to me like you get all of yours and half of mine. I always thought a partnership was fifty-fifty."

"It's not a partnership. You'll be working for me.

I'm furnishing the equipment and taking all the risk. If you lose the traps or give up early, I'm out a lot of money. But if you have a good season, half your catch will amount to quite a bit. A lot more than you can hope to make by hanging around a hardware store. Are you with me?"

"What about food? Who pays for all that?"

"You've been bragging about what a good hunter you are and you said you wanted to live off the land," said Jack. "The place has plenty of fish and birds, and you can shoot a deer to carry you through the cold weather months. I'll furnish salt, sugar, coffee and all the essentials. The rest you'll have to find yourself."

"When would I leave?"

"The fur won't be prime for several months. But you said you wanted to build a cabin and that's going to take some time. You should get started right away so you'll be ready to go by the time it gets cold. If you want to leave now, I can get everything you'll need packed into two canoes. You'll have to paddle and portage them to a spot on Insula that I call Echo Bay. Set up a tent camp a few miles south of there and spend a week exploring."

"After you have your trap lines figured out, pick a central spot and build your cabin. To do it right will take a month or so. By then, it'll be time to trap. I'll be heading out myself in a couple months and I'll stop at Insula and look for the canoes. If you're having problems, put a note in a bottle and stick it under one of the canoes. If everything goes good, you'll trap all fall and when year end comes, pack everything back to Echo Bay. I'll meet you there on New Years Day with a dog sled team and with a couple trips, we'll get all your furs and gear hauled back. When we cash in, you'll be sitting pretty."

"What if New Years comes and you're not there?"

"Don't worry about me. Worry about yourself. Just be at Insula on New Years and everything will be fine."

Mittens was still apprehensive at the thought of doing business with Jack. The more he worked with him, the more he mistrusted him. But when it came to trapping, the guy knew his stuff. He had learned a lot in the few days he worked with him and thought of asking Jack for a bigger share, but he was being offered a chance to fulfill a lifetime dream: building a cabin in the wilderness and living off the land with no one else around except the deer, grouse, rabbits and squirrels. Just thinking about it made him starry eyed. There was no way he could turn the offer down. "Let's get those canoes packed," he said.

Within a few days, they hauled the canoes to the landing and began filling them with gear. Before long, both canoes were crammed to the gunwales with over 100 traps, a canvas tent, iron cook stove, chimney, snowshoes, cold weather clothes, mosquito netting, matches, cookware, rifle, shotgun, ammo and everything else Jack could think of.

"How in the world is one guy going to haul all that stuff?" said Mittens. "If the canoes don't sink from all that weight, it'll take a week to do each portage."

"Don't sweat the canoes. Just be careful not to rock them a lot when you're loaded that heavy, get off the water if you see a storm coming and you'll be fine. Speaking about weight, have you looked in a mirror lately? By the time you're finished with all those portages, you'll have lost so much weight that the canoe will ride higher in the water."

"Very funny," said Mittens as he lifted Millie aboard and pushed the canoes away from the landing. "Just be sure you're there on New Years to bring me back."

"Quit worrying, kid, I'll be there."

With this bit of encouragement, he dipped his paddle into the water and gave it a pull. As he turned back to wave good-bye, his confidence melted. Jack's smile had changed to a sad and wistful look. A look that seemed to say, "We will never meet again."

Chapter 4

Into The Unknown

The heavily loaded canoes floated low in the water and no matter how fast he paddled, the tandem rig had one speed: slow. Jack was right about all the exercise he'd get on the portages. A lot of the gear was tossed in without packsacks and every portage required six or seven round trips. But it was a lot more scenic than walking railroad tracks and he liked the adventurous feel of heading into the unknown.

Late in the day, as he paddled away from the channel that separated Lake 2 and Lake 3, he started looking for a place to camp for the evening. A few hundred yards ahead, a pair of loons were splashing around in the water and he decided to see how close he could get to them. As he paddled closer, both loons dived then popped to the surface 50 feet to his left. He had never seen these funny looking birds before and decided to stop and watch them for awhile.

Millie, who was crammed into a small spot in the canoe by his feet, looked up to see why the paddling had stopped. Spotting the two loons, she jumped up, threw her weight against the left side of the canoe and leaned out over the edge. As the canoe tipped and water began pouring in, Mittens grabbed the dog and yanked her back. As the dog squirmed, he leaned too far to the right and more water poured in from the other side. Finally, he shoved the dog to the floor, locked her between his knees, and waited for the canoe to stop rocking.

When the rocking stopped, he gritted his teeth in anguish as he looked at the sides of the canoe. He had taken on so much water, adding more weight to the already overloaded canoe, that the gunwales were less than an inch above the surface of the water. He was barely afloat and just one more splash from the slightest amount of tipping would send the canoe to the bottom of the lake. And, with the second canoe also overloaded and securely tied to the first, both canoes were in peril.

As the gravity of the situation began to sink in, his mind scrambled for the exit. He was no stranger to trouble, but in the past, there was always someone there to bail him out and if help didn't arrive, he'd simply walk or run from the problem. Now he found himself teetering on the edge of tragedy, not knowing what to do except to stay frozen in position, keep the dog from moving and pray that a large bird didn't fly over and download on the canoe.

This time, yelling for help would do no good and walking away from the problem wasn't an option, so he planned for the worst: the canoes were going down and if he was lucky, some of the gear would float and aid him in his swim for shore. If he was lucky enough to reach shore, and somehow find his way through the wilderness back to Winton, how would he explain to Jack that all the gear is on the bottom of Lake 3?

"No!" he declared, "Somehow, I'm going to get these canoes to shore. I'm not going to sink them." Weighing his options, he thought of tossing gear overboard or trying to release the rope tethering the other canoe. But either action would cause tipping. Bailing out water was the only option. Unable to reach anything that resembled a water container, he carefully removed his shirt, sponged up water from the bottom and wrung the shirt out over the side. After repeating the process many times, the canoe slowly started to ride higher in the water.

With the gunwales now a full inch above water, he stuck the paddle in and gently gave it a pull. While keeping Millie tightly locked between his legs, he slowly turned the canoe, aimed for a nearby island and carefully paddled. After what seemed like an eternity, the canoe bumped into the rocky shore and a rush of relief went through his body when he stepped onto the rocks.

As he off-loaded the gear and started drying it out, he thought, "Darn, I wish Jack could have seen that. After all the lectures he gave me about how I'd have to sharpen my wits if I want to survive and start using intelligence I didn't know I had, he'd be proud of me. Then again, maybe he'd tell me how dumb it is to have a loose dog in an overloaded canoe."

With sunset approaching, he decided to set up camp on the island. Before dark, he made a few casts into the lake and before long, caught a fair sized northern pike. The moon cast long shadows across his campsite and the flickering flame from the fire added a mystical feel. While the fish fillets sizzled in the pan, he thought, "It can't get much better than this."

As morning broke, he pushed the canoes off and continued the journey. After another hard day of paddling and portaging, he spent the night on Hudson Lake, and by the third day, he reached Insula. Paddling to the south end of the lake, he set up a temporary camp on a rock outcrop that overlooked Echo Bay. To make sure this was the bay Jack described, he walked up to the water's edge, cupped his hands around his mouth and yelled, "Hey!" The trees answered back with a "Hey!...Hey!...Hey!...Hey!" Then, he yelled, "Welcome Mittens!" and the forest rolled out a joyous welcome.

After supper, he sat on the shore savoring the moment. The hardships he endured in Hibbing and the scuffle at the railyard were now distant memories. Here in this beautiful place, he controlled his destiny and for the first time in his life, felt contentment and freedom. Alone in the wilderness, he also discovered solitude and loved it. But like other nice things, it came with a price: mosquitoes. Hundreds of the little buggers were swarming around his head, buzzing, biting and trying to ruin his day. Reluctantly he dug out the insect netting

51

from his gear.

The next morning, he filled his packsack with essentials and strung up everything that bears might like. Pulling out a piece of paper, he scrawled a note to Jack:

"Made it here OK. Everything's fine. See you on New Years, Mittens."

Stuffing it in a bottle, he shoved it under one of the canoes.

Before heading into the woods to explore the area, he decided to get a better look at things. Perched on top of a small hill on the other side of the bay was a huge white spruce tree. From its hilltop site, it towered over the forest. He guessed it was over a hundred feet tall and if he climbed it, he'd have a commanding view of the area.

After crossing the bay, he climbed the hill to the base of the tree. It was a whopper all right — almost ten feet in circumference. Best of all, it had a zillion small branches which would make it a breeze to climb. Placing his pack on the ground, he grabbed the branches and started scrambling up. After climbing a short distance, he grabbed a small branch with both hands and when he put his weight onto it, the branch snapped and sent him sliding back down the tree.

As he sat on the soft forest floor, Millie licked his face as if she was trying to bring him around to his senses and make him abandon this foolish endeavor.

But Mittens was determined to climb the tree and when it occurred to him that he would have to keep both hands and both feet on separate branches, instead of placing all his trust on one, he started back up the tree.

He soon found that the tree had a few too many branches. It was like climbing through a jungle. Every few feet, he had to stop and break branches to build a path upward. As he continued the climb, the sharp branches and pin pointed needles started taking a toll on his hands and face which were also building up a coating of tree sap. Stopping to rest, he slapped his face with a sap soaked hand and yelled, "Why am I doing this?" Far below, Millie responded with a low pitched howl, as if urging him to come down. "I didn't go through all this trouble to quit half way up, he mumbled," as he continued the climb.

While looking up and concentrating on keeping a good grip, he didn't notice he had passed and was now above the forest canopy. When he stopped for another rest, the visual shock nearly knocked him off the tree. "Ohmigosh!" he mumbled. Lying before him was a vast sea of green — stretching as far as the eye could see. Clinging to the tree, he stared at the huge expanse in amazement. Mittens wasn't a religious man, but he couldn't help thinking that if there's a heaven, it must look something like this.

After a few moments, he climbed higher to get a view over the remaining tree tops. The trunk was getting smaller and he could feel the tree swaying in the breeze.

"That's high enough," he thought. Pulling a short piece of rope from his pocket, he secured his body to the tree and relaxed his grip.

A year earlier, he had climbed the lookout tower near Hibbing and had a similar view. But for reasons he couldn't understand, this view seemed a lot different — far more dramatic. Perhaps it was because the climb was more difficult, or the feeling of danger greater. Maybe it was the lack of civilization: no roads, no towns, no smokestacks jutting above the horizon. All he could see was an unbroken expanse of green rolling hills — dotted with small depressions that indicated a lake or swamp.

Wiggling around, he moved to the other side of the tree. As he looked out over Lake Insula, he let out another, "Ohmigosh!" The size and beauty of the lake stunned him. The dark blue waters stretched almost to the horizon, broken by occasional bays and small islands. The larger water areas glistened like a diamond nestled in a bed of green. He sat for a long time staring at the striking scene.

Far below, Millie was howling and pawing at the tree, trying to figure out what her master was doing. High above, the wind was picking up speed — increasing the sway. As the swaying intensified, the butterflies in his stomach told him it was time to leave. Unhooking the rope, he started down, carefully retracing his steps until he was safely back on the ground. "You should have seen it." he said to Millie. "It was worth the climb."

Anxious to get a closer look at the sea of green he saw from the treetop, he grabbed his pack and entered the woods. Heading south, he encountered the toughest terrain he had ever seen; The landscape was littered with rocks, and every few yards he had to climb over another fallen tree. It looked like a windstorm had hit the area, causing a large blowdown. The few spots that didn't have obstacles had clusters of alders that were so thick, he almost had to crawl on his hands and knees to get through them.

After a mile, the tough terrain was tempered by occasional rocky ridges — easier to walk, but they all pointed in the wrong direction. As he went up and over each ridge, he ended up back in the thick alders again. Stopping for a rest, he began to get concerned, and thought, "If the whole area is like this, how in the world will I be able to run a trapline?" From his treetop perch, the area looked soft, green and inviting. Up close, however, it was a hard and hostile jungle.

Chapter 5

Paradise Found

The landscape suddenly changed. The brush ended and he was standing in a grove of cedar trees that looked to be more than a hundred years old. He had seen cedars before, but never this big and old, and he had never seen a forest floor like this. Its unbroken span of tight green moss resembled a thick carpet one would expect to see in a fine home. As he stepped on it, his boots sunk slightly, leaving an impression. As he continued walking through this pristine place, he looked back at his tracks and expected to hear someone yell, "Take your boots off!"

Soon, he heard the rushing water of the Ahrnoo Creek. Walking up to the rocky bank, he pulled off his boots and placed his sore feet into the cold clear water.

It felt good. Barefooted, he continued downstream, wading in the shallows and jumping from rock to rock to get across the deep spots. Soon, he reached a large boulder which caused the creek to split into two separate streams that spilled over twin waterfalls before coming together further downstream.

Tired of walking, he stopped to rest by these mystical looking falls. Near the creek was a huge boulder — about 20 feet high. One side had a vertical face that hung over the creek while the backside was angled, facing a small clearing. It was easy to climb the angled side, so he and Millie scooted to the top and sat on a square rock that resembled a chair.

Perhaps it was his happy mood or maybe the relief he felt from finding this small oasis in the wilderness, but as he sat and looked wistfully at the surroundings, he sensed something magical about this spot. That morning, he felt nothing could top the eye-popping view of the island-studded lakes he saw from the treetop. But as awesome as that view was, he felt this place was better.

"If I had to stay in one place the rest of my life," he said, "this would be it."

Scanning the surroundings, something unusual caught his eye: Three boulders were delicately balanced on the edge of the waterfalls. Although they appeared to teeter so loosely that a good wind could blow them over the edge, more than likely they hadn't moved for hundreds, perhaps thousands of years. He had seen a

lot of waterfalls, but none with teetering rocks. That's because most visitors can't resist the urge to push the rocks over the falls and watch them make a big splash.

"Why are those teetering rocks still sitting there?" he thought. "Surely others have visited this place before. Or have they?"

Although the thought seemed absurd, he couldn't help but wonder: "Could I possibly be the first human to visit this beautiful spot? Has anyone else been here before?"

Suddenly, his fantasy was interrupted by Millie's barking. Climbing on the boulder, she looked up at him and barked again. "I guess you want to play ball," he said, as he reached into his pack and pulled out her old ragged baseball. As he flicked his wrist and tossed the ball to the middle of the clearing, the dog scooped it up and quickly brought it back. Each time he threw, he tossed it a bit further until it was bouncing into the trees on the far side of the clearing. The dog found it every time.

He decided to make the game a real challenge. Standing on the boulder, he said, "I'll bet you won't find this one." Then he wound up and threw the ball as hard as he could. It sailed across the creek and bounced into the dense timber on the other side. As Millie raced across the creek and disappeared into the woods, he said, "That'll keep you busy for awhile."

Drifting back into his fantasy, he reached into his

pack and pulled out the night stick he had wrestled away from the railroad cop in Tower. Standing on the rock chair, he stretched out his arm, pointed the stick toward the twin falls and proclaimed, "I, Charles 'Mittens' Perkins declare myself 'King of the Forest' and I claim this land and all its rocks, trees, cliffs and waters to be my kingdom. And I decree that all the birds, fish and animals will be my loyal subjects and they shall obey my command."

Suddenly, the fantasy was interrupted by a terrible howling sound coming from the timber: Millie was in trouble again. Quickly climbing off the boulder and dashing across the creek, he raced to the source of the sound. When he got there, she was groaning in pain. Dozens of porcupine quills were sticking out of her face and she looked like a living pin cushion.

Glancing around the trees, he quickly spotted the problem: a fat old porcupine was treed near the top of a 20-foot aspen. The tree wasn't very big — only three inches in diameter at the base — but Porky looked confident and secure up there.

"No one does that to my dog and gets away with it," he declared. "That fellow looks like he could use a quick lesson in aviation. I'm gonna teach Porky how to fly."

Grabbing the tree, he bent it back as far as he could and let go. The top of the tree whipped forward, but the porcupine hung on.

"OK, so you're gonna be stubborn about it," he said. "Let's see you hang onto this."

Grabbing the tree, he pulled back as hard as he could, then shoved it in the opposite direction. When it was halfway through the sway, he pulled back and the tree top whipped like a cracking bull whip. Porky's back feet went straight out, but his front paws held on like they were glued to the tree. After whipping the tree top several times and failing to dislodge the porcupine, he was out of breath and gasping for air.

After resting a few minutes, he came up with a new plan. "Keep him up there until I get back," he yelled at Millie as he dashed across the creek to get his pack. When he returned, he pulled out a long rope and tied a rock to the end. After spinning the rope around his head a few times, he heaved it at the tree top, making a perfect toss. The rock spun around the tree, just below the porcupine, and he started pulling on the rope.

The plan was simple: he would bend the tree top almost to the ground, then let go of the rope. This would cause the tree to whip forward with so much force that it would launch Porky on a fourth class flight to Lake Insula. Throwing his weight onto the rope, the tree began to bend and the porcupine started to worry. Soon, he had bent the tree into an arc and the top of the tree was nearing the ground. By then, Porky had a plan of his own.

As Mittens kept pulling the tree crown closer, he suddenly felt liquid splashing on his hat. When he looked up, the liquid drenched his face. The porcupine was using his last line of defense: urinating on the aggressor. As Mittens let out a yell and let go of the rope, the porcupine leaped to the ground and ran off into the brush.

Screaming in agony, he raced to the creek. He had tangled with skunks before but nothing could compare to this. He reached the creek and dove in head first, cursing at the top of his lungs and rubbing his face with water. He tried scrubbing with sand, dirt and leaves, but nothing would stop the itching and burning. After several grueling minutes, the itching eased but the smell remained.

Most of the odor came from his clothes, so he removed them and scrubbed them on the rocks. While waiting for them to dry, he started pulling quills out of Millie's face. Each one had barbs like a fishhook and the dog howled even harder as he yanked them out. Finally he gave up and decided to let them fall out on their own. From that day forth, the "King of the Forest" gave porcupines a wide berth when they met in the woods.

Chapter 6

Home Sweet Home

After camping overnight, he started exploring the area for places to trap. Following the Ahmoo Creek, he spotted a few active beaver ponds and marked them on his map. South of the Ahmoo were numerous small creeks and swamps. "Jack knew what he was doing when he picked this area," he thought. "Even a beginner like me can do well here." As he continued exploring and mapping, he started counting the money he was going to make. As the day wore on, he arrived at Arrow Lake near the east side of the permit area.

Tired from all the hiking that day, he stopped and set up an overnight camp on a hill by the lake. "There's lots of daylight left. Let's go catch us some supper," he said to Millie as he headed for the lake. After crawling

Mittens In The Boundary Waters

down a steep wooded bank, he entered a thick stand of black spruce that were growing in green spongy ground that looked like tundra. As he continued through the spruce, the trees started to thin and he failed to notice they leaned and moved with each step he took. Soon, the trees ended and he walked up to the water's edge. Looking down, he noticed how dark the water was and when he wiggled his body, the water would ripple. "How strange," he thought.

Setting his pack down, he pulled out his fishing rod, stuck on a lure and made a few casts. After awhile, nothing was biting so he decided to try a different spot. Suddenly, he spotted a fish, just below the surface swimming toward him. Instead of turning when it reached shore, it continued under his feet. "This is really weird," he thought. "I think I'll check the water depth."

Bending down, he pushed his fishing rod into the water, but couldn't touch bottom. Walking back to the trees, he broke off an eight foot tall dead spruce, returned to shore and shoved the tree in the water. After pushing it nearly all the way down, he still couldn't touch bottom. Suddenly, it occurred to him that he was on a floating bog — thick enough to support the small trees and give the illusion of being close to shore. In reality, he was a long way from shore.

"Yikes!" he thought. "If a chunk of this bog breaks off, I'll be in water over my head." Gently picking up his pack and gear, he carefully tip toed back to the true shoreline. As he stood there thinking, he suddenly had an idea and walked back to the place where the trees started to thin. Pulling out his knife, he jabbed it into the bog and cut a one foot diameter circle. After a bit of digging and clawing, he yanked out the round plug of bog and sure enough, there was open water below it.

"There's no place for you to hide now," he said, as he tossed the lure in the hole. It didn't take long and the line snapped tight — he had a fish. Slowly he pulled it towards the hole, reached in and yanked it out. It was a northern pike — almost two feet long. He hurriedly threw the lure in and caught another one. For unknown reasons, the northerns liked to hang out under the floating bog. "This is crazy," he thought. "I'm ice fishing in the middle of summer."

After catching a third one, he covered the hole with brush and returned to camp. After cleaning the fish and frying one of them, the worries he had about finding enough food to eat in the wilderness started fading and he began to worry that he was going to get too fat in this land of plenty.

At dawn, he was on his way again. After locating several good trapping sites on the east side of Arrow Lake, he started a wide zigzag hike to the west, mapping the best spots between Arrow and Pose Lake. He decided on two circular trapping routes which resembled butterfly wings. By locating his cabin in the center, he could make a one day sweep of each route and be back at the cabin every night.

After a lot of looking, he selected a spot on the

north edge of a large open swamp — bordered by a low rocky ledge. The cabin would face the clearing to take advantage of warming from the sun and it wasn't too far from his fishing hole on Arrow Lake. To help block the wind, he decided to build the cabin below the rock ledge on the swampy ground. If it flooded in the spring, it would be no problem because he planned to be gone by New Years.

BUILDING HIS DREAM HOME

The creek that connected Arrow Lake to Insula wasn't canoeable, so he hacked a trail through the two miles of wilderness back to Lake Insula. After several back-breaking, mosquito slapping trips, all the gear was at the cabin site and his temporary camp was complete. He also figured out a way to win the mosquito war: get out of bed early. Since mosquitoes are late sleepers, he found that by rising early he could have nearly a days work done before the little buggers were out of bed.

At first light, he was in high spirits, sharpening his tools and making plans for the cabin. Wanting lots of room, he prepared the ground for a 16' X 20' building. The nearby jack pines would work nicely, but he wanted to leave them for shade, so he selected a group of pines a few hundred feet from camp. Picking out a nice straight tree with a one foot diameter trunk, he pulled out his axe.

The first blow sunk the axe so deeply into the tree that he had to wiggle the handle to get it out. The next one hit at an angle just above the first and a large chip of wood flew. "This is going to be a breeze," he thought. As he continued swinging, his arms tired and the swings became less accurate, often requiring ten swings to dislodge a single chip of wood. His hands — tender from clerking in a hardware store — soon started blistering. Donning his gloves to slow the soreness, he continued whacking away at the tree until it finally crashed to the ground. "At this rate, It'll take me two years," he thought.

Adding two feet to allow for corners, he used a crosscut saw to cut the log to length. After trimming the branches from the 22' log, he grabbed it and gave a yank. It felt like it was glued to the ground. After pushing, rolling, grunting and groaning, it occurred to him that he'd need a horse or a bulldozer to skid the log 200 feet to the cabin site. And even if he figured a way to move the logs, he'd never be able to lift them into place.

There was only one answer: make the cabin smaller. After convincing himself there would be more charm to a 16' X16', he shortened the log to 18'. It still felt like it was bolted to the ground when he tried to move it. As the day wore on, he convinced himself that the quaintness of a cabin that measured only 9' X 7' inside was what he truly wanted; Wide enough for his bed and enough extra room for the stove and dog. Most of the supplies could be tucked into the rafters.

Shortening the logs speeded up the process and in a few weeks the walls were up and the roof trusses in

place. With side walls only five feet high, the door opening was shrunk to 3' X 3". "I guess I'll have to crawl in each time," he thought. "But a small door means it will be easier to heat." To make room inside to stand up, he spaced the roof trusses to leave an open area in the middle.

After felling a cedar tree, he sawed the log in short chunks and split each piece several times to make shake shingles for roofing. When the roof was complete, he started whittling out a door. Concerned about bears breaking in, he made it out of large log stubs and spent days shaping it to a wedge type fit. The door would swing out to open and if you tried to push it in, as a bear would do, it would wedge tighter into the frame. When the door was finished, it fit perfectly and opened and closed with ease. He was proud of his craftsmanship, but failed to realize that an outward swinging door can be a tragic mistake in a wilderness cabin.

The final job was sealing all the openings. Mittens hated mice and Jack had told him a few horror stories of how they invade wilderness cabins in the winter. Unwilling to share space with these tiny furry friends, he figured out a way to "mouseproof" the place. Remembering a place by the Ahmoo Creek where his feet got bogged down in sticky blue clay, he decided to get some of that gooey stuff and use it as a sealer. Using his trap boiling bucket, he made several trips to the creek, hauling back clay.

The first coat filled the gaps between the logs. After smearing it on, he let it dry a day then continued building up the layers. After a few days, cracks formed which he filled with lighter coats until he had a tight seal. The clay worked so well on the walls that he also used it on the roof. When completed, his dream cabin resembled a mud structure that one would see over in Africa. Although this insult to north woods architecture wasn't the charming wilderness cabin he envisioned, it answered his concerns about mice, bears and keeping warm in the winter. He was proud of it.

To store food, he dug a large hole next to the cabin, lined it with logs and built a tightly sealed cover out of heavy logs. With strong leather hinges on one side and a heavy wire tie down on the other, it would take a pretty big bear to bust into it. With the food box and cabin completed, he started work on the hide racks and cabin furniture. For a finishing touch, he carved "C.M.P. 1931" above the door.

As summer came to an end he discovered another new entree to add to his menu: blueberries. They were popping up in nearly every swampy area and each day he headed in a different direction carrying a large bag. After several hours picking, he'd have the bag full, eat a generous helping and store the rest in his food box to eat later. His favorite recipe was filling a bowl half full of berries, mash them up and add water and sugar.

Millie wasn't very fond of fish and berries, but that wasn't a problem. She was getting so adept at catching mice and other small critters, that she rarely needed to be fed. With his newly found diet of berries, supplemented by fish and an occasional grouse, he was putting on weight fast. Too fast. He was becoming concerned that he was getting out of condition for the upcoming rigors of working the trapline.

Chapter 7

The Trapping Begins

As the months rolled by, he felt the chill of autumn in the air. The fur would soon be at its prime and it was time to set traps. Starting on the east circle, he built a crude trail that would reach all of the sets and bring him back to the cabin by dark. Halfway through each circle, he constructed emergency lean-to structures in case he couldn't complete the circle route in a day. After building both routes, he started making the sets.

Carefully following Jack's instructions, the trapline started producing immediately. Even though he was up every morning before dawn, he still couldn't keep up and had to idle many traps. Hauling that many animals back to the cabin each day was back breaking work. And the day wasn't done when he got back. He had to work far into the night skinning the animals, making stretchers and getting them hung up. Then there was the small matter of eating. It was too early to shoot a deer because of warm weather spoilage, so he had to find time to hunt grouse and catch fish. He never dreamed that running a trapline would be this much work, but thinking about the payday in January made it a lot easier.

November came and with it came snow. As he walked through the woods, the glistening snow that blanketed the trees and shrubs felt cold and forbidding. It was also deathly quiet in the woods. Without the leaves crunching under his feet, he walked in almost total silence. The only sound was the occasional cawing of a raven and the soft patter of Millie's feet prancing behind him.

The drastic change caused by the snow made him feel like he was in a different place. A place far different from that of summer. He'd seen his share of snow during his winters in Minnesota, but the change in season was never this dramatic. When it snowed in town, you'd hardly notice it; roads and sidewalks were quickly cleared and life went on as usual. Here in the wilderness, the change was hard to ignore.

Something else felt different: Perhaps it was the feeling of being alone in the woods that caused it, but as the days wore on he had a strange feeling that he was being watched. He didn't know why he felt that way, but he was almost certain that someone or something was watching him.

WALKING A TIGHTROPE

The temperature was falling and the snow was getting deep as he left his cabin to work the east route around Arrow Lake. The heavy snow covered his trap sets, causing delays and as nightfall neared, he was still on the east side of the lake — only halfway through the route. He hadn't stocked the emergency camps with food and supplies yet and would have to return to the cabin. He groaned as he thought about the long hike around the lake he'd have to take to get back.

Arrow is shaped like an hour glass: two bodies of water connected in the middle by a small creek. He was close to the creek and if it had frozen over, he could walk a straight line back to the cabin. This would save at least an hour of walking and he might reach the cabin before dark. He decided to give it a try.

Arriving at the creek, he was disappointed to find that the current was preventing it from freezing. After following it north and south, he couldn't find a rock crossing, but found a wide place in a wooded area that was iced over. As he stepped onto the ice, it started to crack from his weight, so he backed off.

Having wasted a lot of time searching for a crossing, he now had a new problem: If he went back to the trapline, the walk around the lake would now be in darkness. Without a moon, it would be a tough task. But if he could somehow get across the creek, there

was a chance of reaching the cabin before dark.

He decided to test the ice further. As he stepped on, it sagged, but as he walked further into the trees, it became solid. Continuing on, the ice alternately switched from solid to weak. Soon, the trees ended and he reached a large rock next to the main part of the creek and climbed onto it. Standing safely on the rock, he stared at the wide expanse of ice ahead of him until he got his courage up and started across. But as the ice creaked and sagged, he panicked and quickly returned to the safety of the rock.

With the temperature hovering near zero, falling through the ice could be life threatening and he had no idea if the water was only a couple feet deep, or over his head. He knew the ice was safe where he started, but wasn't sure how strong it would be in the middle of the creek. Feeling it wasn't worth the risk, he turned and started back to the trapping trail.

"Here I go again," he thought. "I walk away from trouble rather than facing it and finding a solution." Now that he was on his own, this slow thinker was slowly developing a talent for clear thinking. Suddenly, he remembered an incident from his childhood: It was early winter and his friends were taking turns scampering across the thin ice of a creek near the school. He was heavier than his friends and didn't want to try it, but they kept egging him on until he did. As he walked slowly and cautiously across the ice, it suddenly broke and he fell in up to his waist. Since then, he was scared

79

of ice.

"Why didn't I run quick and take short steps like the others?" he thought. "The reason I fell in was probably because I was being too slow and cautious." Turning around, he headed back to the creek.

He had a plan: Grabbing a few large stones, he heaved them into the air, causing them to drop at various places on the ice. Each stone bounced off the ice — indicating that there were no thin spots. Then, he removed his heavy pack, attached a long rope to it, tied a stone to the end of the rope and threw it across the creek. Using short and quick running steps, he planned to scamper across the ice and when he reached the other side, he'd grab the rope, drag the pack across and continue on his way.

Stepping off the rock, he assumed a crouching position and rehearsed the quick steps he'd take on his 50 foot dash to the other side. After several false starts, he couldn't do it and stepped back on the rock. Millie looked at him in bewilderment, wondering what he was doing. He imagined that she was calling him a big chicken.

When his courage returned, he stepped off the rock and onto the ice again. His heart was pounding and his knees were knocking, but this time, there would be no turning back. It had become a matter of pride. Was he a rough and tough woodsman, or was he a wimp? "I am Charles 'Mittens' Perkins, King of the Forest," he yelled. "No small creek is going to stop me!" Then he let out another yell and charged out onto the ice.

The ice started to sag, but he had reached the point of no return and knew that if he stopped or tried to turn around, he'd fall through. Moving his feet as fast as he could, he reached the other side and dashed into the bushes. Raising his hands high, he let out a victory yell, then called to Millie to come across.

He was so elated at crossing the creek that he overlooked a small detail: he wasn't completely across and what he thought was dry land was still ice. Suddenly the ice gave way and he fell into the water up to his hips. While cursing his stupidity, he tried to move but his feet were stuck in the sticky creek bottom. After twisting and turning awhile, his right foot popped loose and as he struggled to free the other foot, his boot came off. He could now move freely, but if he didn't retrieve the stuck boot, it would be a grueling hike back to camp.

After failing to get his foot back in the boot, he waded over to the rope, pulled the pack across and dug out his trapping hoe. With the weather that cold, he couldn't risk getting more of his body wet, so he gingerly stuck the hoe in the water and hooked the boot. Yanking on it with one hand, he couldn't pull it loose, so he stuck both arms in the water, gripped the hoe firmly and twisted it until the boot came free.

Grabbing his pack, he struggled through the muck and crawled onto solid ground. He had finally crossed the creek, but he paid a price: over half his body was soaking wet. With the sun down and the temperature falling, he knew he had to get to the cabin as fast as he could. Stashing his pack by the creek, he took off in the direction of camp at a slow jog that soon turned into a sluggish walk as the alders got thicker and his pants began to freeze.

The woods turned black and the stars shined bright as he struggled through the darkness. He had no light or compass and kept his course by glancing at the North Star. As he tripped on the rocks and stumbled through the brush, his ice encrusted legs begged him to stop and build a fire. But in his haste to leave the creek, he left his matches in the pack and had no choice but to continue.

Suddenly, he reached a steep hill. So steep that he had to crawl on all fours to climb it. He had almost reached the top, when he slipped, rolled all the way back down and landed in a snowbank. Lying on his back in the soft snow, he was exhausted. He had to rest.

As he laid on his back, he looked up at the bright glow of the stars. A gentle breeze made the jack pines sway, and as the branches crossed the sky, it caused the stars to flicker. Slowly he started to feel warm and happy. He knew this was wrong and he knew he had to leave — right now. But happiness had always been an elusive pursuit for him. He wanted to savor this treasured moment just a little longer.

Suddenly, he felt a splash; Millie was licking his face. "OK old partner," he said. "Let's try that hill again."

His pants and sleeves were frozen solid and made a crunching sound when he stood up. With his energy renewed, he attacked the hill again, reached the top and scrambled down the other side. He was back in familiar territory and soon reached the cabin. After firing up the stove and wrestling off his frozen clothes, he checked his feet. It was close, but they would be OK. With the smell of grouse sizzling on the stove, he patted Millie's head and wondered, "If she hadn't licked my face, would I still be laying in the snow by that hill?

Chapter 8

Meeting The Enemy

The next morning his body was stiff and sore as he crawled out of bed and prepared for another long day on the trapline. His first project would be to retrieve his pack by Arrow Lake. After locating the pack, he walked to the spot where he fell in the water the night before. Tapping his foot on the ice, he checked the thickness. The temperature had dropped below zero during the night and the ice was now rock solid.

Again, he was faced with the problem of crossing. If he could cross at this spot, he'd quickly be back on his trapline. If not, he'd have to circle the lake and waste several hours getting to the other side. The ice held him last night — sort of. With the extra freezing, it surely would be safe now. But looking at the creek still made

85

his veins tingle.

Deciding he had bathed enough to last for the next few weeks, he decided to take the long way around. By late morning, he was near the floating bog fishing hole, so he decided to stop and thin out the school of fish a bit more. The hole was frozen shut, but after a bit of chopping, he had it open and tossed in a line.

This time he wasn't having any luck. After an hour of poking the line around and trying different lures, he concluded that the fish had gone into hibernation. It troubled him a bit because the fishing spot had been so reliable. Just like shopping in a grocery store, it had faithfully produced fish for months. Now there was nothing. "Oh well," he thought. "I was getting tired of eating fish anyway."

When he reached the trapline, he found he had caught three more beaver in the sets he placed the day before and couldn't believe the luck he was having. After hauling them back to camp, he cleaned, stretched and hung the hides, then broke out another can of blueberries from the huge stash he had put aside in late summer. "Who needs fish, when I've got these, "he thought. "And soon, I'll be eating venison."

The next morning was crisp, cold and sunny as he left camp and headed out on the west trapping route. The snow was starting to build up, but not to the point of requiring snowshoes. By now, he had walked the two routes so many times that they were nearly free of brush and the snow was hard packed from the regular footsteps. He could cruise the trails with ease.

The strange feeling that he was being "watched" was particularly strong that day. Even Millie seemed uneasy and kept stopping to look around. He continued to feel that it was caused by the quiet of the winter forest, but like the dog, he felt uneasy and kept glancing over his shoulder.

By mid day, halfway through the trapping route, the cause for concern showed itself. Out of nowhere, a large timberwolf appeared. Mittens was startled; he couldn't figure out where it came from. But there it was, standing in the trail — just 30 feet away — facing him and blocking the path.

He had never seen anything like this before. The wolf was a big black male that probably weighed over 100 pounds and it looked mean and dangerous. The most frightening feature was the eyes: gold in color, stern and piercing, they were the eyes of the devil. As the animal stared at him, it sent chills down his spine. Until now, he had a misguided fantasy that he was the master of the forest and feared nothing. As the wolf lowered his head and uttered a low pitched growl, the fantasy crumbled into reality. He was facing the real master and he was scared.

As Millie started forward, he quickly grabbed her collar and held on. Jack had assured him there would be no problem with wolves — they seldom attack humans. But he wasn't too sure about the dog. "Is it possible that the wolf resents Millie invading his territory?" he thought. The dog was twisting and squirming — trying to slip out of her collar. Mittens kneeled down and locked her securely between his knees. When he looked up again, the wolf was gone. He was astonished. He had looked away for only a few seconds, and like a ghost, the wolf disappeared into the brush.

Rather than continue ahead and risk another encounter, he turned around and headed back to camp. The encounter left him scared, trembling and constantly glancing back to see if the wolf was following. After walking the trail for awhile, his nerves settled down and he regained his composure.

With his confidence returning, he thought about turning around and resuming the trapline. After all, the wolf episode was more than likely a rare encounter — unlikely to happen again. "That wolf is probably more scared than me," he thought. "He's probably in the next county by now." It was a nice thought, but it was wishful thinking.

After walking for 20 minutes, confident that he was far away from the wolf, he found a small clearing by the trail, sat down on a fallen tree and took a break. As he petted the dog, he noticed she was restless and excited, as if the wolf was still there. "That nasty old wolf is gone," he said. "He's not going to bother us anymore." But the dog kept squirming; something was bothering her.

Out the corner of his eye, he caught a slight movement deep in the woods. As he took a harder look, terror raced through him — the wolf was back. To make matters worse, now there were two of them: a smaller gray female had joined up. He couldn't tell if there were more than two and didn't really care. All he could think about was getting out of there.

Fearing Millie would try to chase them, he grabbed a short piece of rope from his pack and tethered the dog to his belt. Without taking his eyes off the wolves, he slowly put his pack on and gingerly headed down the trail. Soon, he was out of the clearing and out of the wolves' sight.

Hiking nervously along the trail, his head was constantly moving as he tried to look in every direction. Each time he approached a bush or boulder, he expected a wolf to leap out from behind. He cursed himself for not carrying his rifle, but it would have been extra weight for his already overloaded pack and he felt he only needed to carry a gun when he was looking for food. Right now, his only means of defense was a large skinning knife and a policeman's night stick. As he gripped the knife in his hand, he wasn't sure how he'd use it if they attacked, but at least it gave him a small amount of confidence.

Suddenly, he saw a flash in the woods — 100 feet to the right. Then he saw it again. It was the black wolf, sneaking through the woods like an apparition. Mittens stepped up the pace to a brisk walk — almost a jog.

The wolf stayed slightly ahead of him, occasionally stopping to watch him and the dog pass. Each time he caught a glimpse of the wolf, he quickened his pace and soon, he was running. He thought he was a hunter, but now he was the "hunted"!

There was only one thought on his mind: get back to the safety of the cabin. As he hurried along, he reached the final ridge separating him from camp. Scrambling to the top of the ridge, he paused and looked down. Only one obstacle remained: a swamp with black spruce so thick, you couldn't see ten feet in front of you. His trapping trail wound tightly through those trees and if the wolves were going to ambush him, it would be the perfect place.

With the cabin on the other side of the spruce swamp, he decided it would be safer to circle the swamp and stay out of the dense timber. This meant tougher walking and a longer route, but it would be safer than the other way. After climbing down the hill, he headed for the open timber. Rounding the swamp, he spotted the cabin and with his pulse racing, took off in a run.

When he got within 50 yards of the cabin, he stopped in his tracks. The wolves had reached the cabin first. The gray wolf was standing by the rocky ledge, ten feet from the door and the black wolf was sneaking around behind the cabin. A strange "face-off" began. Walking to an open area, he sat down and waited for the wolves to leave.

After waiting a while, he started getting cold. He had perspired so much during the frantic hike that his clothing was wringing wet and starting to freeze. Darkness was getting closer and the wolves wouldn't leave. They seemed content to sit and wait for him and the dog to come to them.

While he sat and shivered, he weighed his options: If he stayed in this spot longer, he'd have to build a fire by a nearby boulder to warm up. With the boulder covering his backside and the fire in front, the wolves would probably leave him alone. But the thought of spending a cold night in the woods while in plain view of his cozy cabin was annoying. And if the wolves wanted to attack, why hadn't they done it by now?

Racking his brain, he struggled for an answer. Perhaps the wolves were simply hungry. Maybe the animal odors from his trap pack were exciting them. Maybe if he gave them something to eat, they would go away. Reaching into his pack, he pulled out a chunk of meat. He decided to enter camp and if the wolves didn't leave, he'd throw the meat at them and make a dash for the cabin.

With darkness approaching, he summoned his courage and began walking toward the camp. When he got close, the gray wolf jumped up on the ledge by the cabin door and uttered a low pitched growl — daring him to come closer. She wasn't as big and wild looking as the black wolf. In fact, she resembled a large German shepherd dog. But when she growled — exposing her large canines — it was clear that this was no dog.

When he got within 30 feet of the cabin, he held the chunk of meat up, twirled it around so the wolves would get the scent, then gave it a toss. It landed on the ledge a few feet from the gray wolf. The black wolf scooted out from behind the cabin, scooped up the snack and left, but the gray wolf ignored the meat and held her ground.

Mittens had one thought: get inside the cabin. Millie was getting hysterical and pulling hard on the tether rope. With his knife in one hand and the other restraining the dog, he walked to within 20 feet of the wolf, made a wide swing around her and inched his way closer to the cabin door. Each time Millie struggled to break free, the wolf threatened to leap off the rock ledge and attack. Again, he wondered, "Is the wolf after me, or my dog?" When he got within five feet of the cabin, he lunged for the door, swung it open, shoved the dog inside and dove in after her. As he secured the door behind him, he let out a sigh of relief.

Reaching into the rafters, he pulled out the rifle, filled the magazine with cartridges and slowly opened the door. Crawling halfway through the doorway, he glanced around camp but couldn't see them. "Are wolves smart enough to flee at the sight of a gun?" he thought. "They can't be that smart. They're probably hiding behind a bush or in back of the cabin, waiting for me to come out so they can get me." Crawling back into the cabin, he bolted the door shut.

Darkness was enveloping the camp as he started cooking supper. His hands were still trembling as he thought about the events of the day. He had seen wolves in a zoo and they didn't look that frightening. He had a few encounters with mean dogs when he was young and it didn't bother him. But this was different: there was no fence separating them and these weren't just dogs. They were savage beasts.

Suddenly, he heard a sound outside — like a stick breaking. "They're back," he thought. "Will they try to break in?" After double checking the latch on the door, he huddled quietly in the corner and listened for more sounds. But the sounds never came except in the fertile imagination of his mind.

In this remote area — far from civilization — he was on his own. With no one else around, it was his private domain. He was in charge and no one told him what he could or couldn't do. The forest was his friend, but more than that, it was a place of security. He had always felt safe in the woods, but not anymore. Without taking a bite, the wolves had ripped away his cloak of confidence, slashed his brazen false sense of security and left him cowering in the corner of his cabin.

Following a long night of fitful sleep laced with nightmares about wolves, morning came and he opened the door. Carefully peeking out, he couldn't spot the enemy; the coast was clear. He still didn't relish the idea of going out on the trapline and facing the wolves again, so he stayed in the cabin most of the day. By late

93

afternoon, necessity forced him to go outside and chop firewood. Following each swing of the axe, he looked over his shoulder to see if a wolf was sneaking up. They were beginning to run his life.

That night, he managed to put things into perspective and thought, "This is crazy. If the wolves plan to attack, why didn't they do it yesterday? Are they afraid of me? All I know for sure is that I'll have to learn to cope with them so I can get back on the trapline." He decided to give it a try in the morning.

The next day, he stepped outside, confident that the wolves wouldn't bother him. But to be on the safe side, he decided to work the east route — away from the wolves. He also starting carrying his rifle. He didn't like the extra weight, but he liked the extra peace of mind.

As an added safety measure, he decided to leave Millie behind, locked in the cabin. By now, she was accustomed to his routine of loading the pack in preparation for the daily hike and it didn't take long for her to figure out what he planned to do. She wanted no part of it, but after a bit of struggling, he stuffed her into the cabin and blocked the door.

Hefting up his pack, he headed out on the trapline. After walking a few yards, the dog started howling, clawing at the door and making a big racket while trying to get out. He hollered at her a few times, but the commotion continued until he gave in and let her come along. He was worried she might wreck things inside the cabin and her noise could draw in wolves. Besides, he had become so accustomed to her trotting behind him that things wouldn't seem the same without her. But to be on the safe side, he put her tether rope on.

Chapter 9

The Deer Hunter

After walking all day without spotting wolf tracks, his fear of the wolves was starting to ease. He even felt comfortable freeing Millie from her tether and letting her run free. But his pleasure over the lack of wolf tracks was offset by the lack of a different kind of track: deer tracks. He hadn't paid attention since the snow came, but now he noticed that there were few, if any, deer in the area.

If he were in the woods near Hibbing, there would be tracks everywhere. But for reasons unknown to him, this area hardly had any. A week earlier, he saw deer tracks that were several days old, but nothing fresh. It was November and there should be antler rubs on the trees, buck scrapes on the ground and deer droppings

97

everywhere.

It was critical to have a food supply to sustain him through the cold months of November and December and he had counted on having his locker stocked with venison. Of course, getting a deer would be simple. He expected to see a lot of them while working the trapline and planned to pick out a nice fat one, then cull it from the herd — close to camp, of course, so he wouldn't have to drag it very far.

Now he was a bit uncertain. It was well into November, his food supply at the cabin was getting lean and he was reaching a point where having the venison was more important than trapping. Feeling he had no other choice, he decided to trip the traps and hunt until he bagged a deer.

Back at the cabin, he hunched over the map and planned his strategy. It was clear he had to leave the area and find a place where there were more deer. If he headed north, he'd bump into a lot of large lakes and have trouble traveling. Except for a few river crossings, it appeared that traveling south would be a breeze. He could pack for overnight and hike several miles until he found deer country. It would take a lot of walking, but by removing the trapping gear from his pack and carrying only his rifle, overnight gear and a few cooking utensils, the pack would be manageable. The decision was made: head south and don't return without a deer.

The morning sun was peeking through the pines as he and Millie left the cabin and headed south. The lighter weight of the pack made a big difference when he climbed hills or went through heavy brush. And, after weeks of lugging a fully loaded pack around the trapline, the fat around his waist was disappearing and his legs felt like steel pillars. He was developing muscles he never knew he had.

The goal for the day was to hunt and hike south until he reached Lake Isabella and then set up a temporary camp. As he left the familiar area of the traplines and hiked into new and strange surroundings, he started following the ridge tops, checking for deer sign and adjusting his course to maintain a south heading.

After hiking all day, he noticed light showing through the trees ahead. As he topped a ridge, a large white expanse stretched out before him: Lake Isabella. The lake looked cold and forbidding while locked in its prison of ice and snow. He imagined that when summer came, it was probably as pretty as Insula, but it was hard to see the beauty in it now.

With only a few hours of daylight left, he located a small open area and started to make a temporary camp. He hadn't seen any deer sign during the day and doubted if he'd remain in the area, but he would need a place that night and also on the return trip, so he spent extra time making a deluxe camp. Attaching a long limb between two trees for a ridge, he leaned several dozen limbs against it to form a lean-to. To tame the wind, he stuffed the sides and top with spruce boughs, then built a large bed using soft white pine boughs.

As he finished hauling in a supply of firewood and building a fire pit, darkness came and soon he was sitting by the fire, slowly basting one of the grouse he had bagged that day. As the moon came up from behind the trees, it cast shadows across the camp, lending a magic touch to the setting. Since the snow came, he had avoided camping outside. Fearing a cold and miserable night, he had always managed to get back to his cabin for the evening. But now he felt different. He was warm and cozy by the fire and the view of the evening sky was a welcome break from looking at a cabin ceiling. "Ain't this the life?" he said to Millie as he crawled into his sleeping bag and dozed off.

As the morning sun came up, Millie licked his face to wake him. It was time to resume the hunt, but he had other ideas that morning. Ever since his fishing hole on Arrow Lake dried up, he longed for fresh northerns. Looking out over Lake Isabella, he wondered if there were fish in it. He decided that the hunt would have to wait. Right now, he had fishing on his mind.

Hiking down to the shore, he looked at the wide expanse and shook his head. He had no idea where to look for fish, and he wasn't sure if the ice was safe. Following the shoreline west, he arrived at a small bay. "This is where the fish will be," he said. Whether he believed that or not, was secondary. He wanted a place where he could swim back to shore if he fell through the ice.

100

Stepping onto the lake, he stopped to kick away the snow exposing the ice. It was rock solid and took several strikes with his hatchet to break through. Confident the ice would hold, he hiked to the middle of the bay, cleared a wide patch of snow and chopped a hole in the ice.

Although he outfoxed the northerns on Arrow Lake, blind luck would be his biggest ally on this unfamiliar lake. Huddled in a blanket to block the wind, he patiently watched the line, pulling it out every 10 minutes and trying something different from his box of lures. After several hours, he quit in disgust and returned to shore. While building a fire and thawing out, he thought of giving up fishing and concentrate on the more important job of hunting. But determined to have fish for supper, he headed back onto the ice and tried again.

As the hours passed, he tried every lure he had and when that didn't work, he tried setting the lures at different depths. As the afternoon wore on, he was getting cold, disgusted and ready to quit. After changing lures one more time and making another depth adjustment, his line suddenly twitched. After feeding more line into the hole, he gave the rod a jerk. The hook set and he had a northern on the line — a big one. After several minutes, he worked it toward the hole, pulled it out and let out a yell. He had never caught a fish this big before and guessed that it weighed over ten pounds.

"I wish I could show this one to Mrs. Larsen," he

thought. "She'd probably accuse me of buying it at the grocery store."

The northern was big enough for a couple meals, but now that he had the formula figured out, he wasn't about to quit. The big fish had pumped up his adrenalin and he wasn't cold anymore. With an hour of daylight remaining, he tossed the lure back in the water. Soon, he had another and by the time the sun set, he had caught five. The last four weren't as big as the first one, but big enough to keep him supplied with food for quite awhile.

After dragging the fish back to shore, he decided to store a few to eat on the return trip. After cleaning them, he laid a bunch on the ice and packed them in snow. Working under the moonlight, he cut another hole in the ice, dipped water out and poured it on the pile of fish. As the water froze, he continued pouring more until it formed a hard shell which would be tough for animals to break. Finally, he covered it with a pile of snow.

After marking the cache so he could find it later, he headed back to the temporary camp to make supper. It had been a long time since he savored the smell of fresh northern frying in a pan. Grouse was OK, but only blueberries could top this treat. The dog wasn't very fond of fish, so Mittens ate it all himself, except for some he saved for breakfast. "Tomorrow we're gonna have venison." he said to Millie as he cleaned up the frying pan.

102

Calling it a day, he crawled into his sleeping bag, sank into the soft pine bed and thought about his problems. He was worried he wouldn't get a deer and was still concerned that wolves would return to his trapping area. But now a third problem was emerging: the solitude was starting to wear on him.

He missed swapping stories with his friends and keeping up with the latest gossip in town. He thought about Louise and how wonderful it would be to hear her sweet voice again. After months without seeing another human, the loneliness was troubling and he was thankful he brought his dog along. Even though she couldn't talk, a one way conversation was better than nothing. Solitude was fine, but he didn't care for such a big dose and was counting the days until New Years when he could talk to people again.

Chapter 10

A Stranger In The Woods

A thick morning fog hung over the camp as he crawled out of bed. It was so thick that it blocked the sun and cast a gloom over the forest. After breakfast, he headed west along the lake and into the deep woods. The brush in the area wasn't dense and he was able to cover a lot of ground while searching for deer tracks. After a few hours, however, he hadn't found a single one and except for occasional squirrel tracks, the area seemed devoid of wildlife. The heavy haze was still lingering in the air — hiding the sun and making the woods feel creepy. He wished he'd have picked that day for fishing and hunted the day before when it was sunny.

The relentless quest to find deer sign continued

for several more hours. As he strutted along, reality began to set in: there were no deer in the area and he'd have to try a different place. Suddenly, as he rounded the edge of a muskeg swamp, he glanced at the ground and yelled, "Ohmigosh!" There in the snow ahead of him were tracks. Not deer tracks, but human tracks — fresh ones. At first, he couldn't believe it. Surely his eyes were playing tricks on him. But as he bent down to take a closer look, he became a believer. Someone else was in the woods.

His first thought was ,"It must be Jack. He's come to pick me up."

Then he thought, "No, that's not possible. He's not due for a month, and we're supposed to meet at Lake Insula, not way down here."

Excitedly, he started following the tracks, but after a short time a troubling thought occurred to him: "Am I heading into trouble? What if the guy I'm following is some type of wild man or hermit who lives in the wilderness and hates people? He may not take kindly to my invasion of his territory. Should I just leave him alone?"

But his urge to see another person, to talk to someone — anyone — was so overwhelming that it clouded his thinking. He didn't care if the guy he was following was Jack the Ripper. He desperately wanted to talk to him and hear another human voice. Plodding forward, he hastily followed the tracks.

106

After trotting along for awhile, he noticed from the size of the tracks that the fellow had about the same size feet as he did. And, it appeared that he also had a dog.

"Anybody who owns a dog, can't be all that bad," he thought, as he increased his speed to a jog. Every few minutes he stopped, cupped his hands on his mouth and yelled, "Wait! Stop." But the person he was following wouldn't stop or respond to his calls. Mittens refused to give up and relentlessly continued the pursuit.

As he followed the tracks through the overcast forest, he suddenly noticed something different: a second person had joined up with the fellow he was following. Now he was following two people.

"It has to be a group of deer hunters," he thought. "But why would there be hunters way out here by Lake Isabella? How did they get here? And what kind of hunter is dumb enough to bring a dog along on a deer hunting trip?"

A thought was entering his mind that was hard to dismiss, so he stopped and studied the footprints again. Placing his foot next to the tracks, he observed that both sets matched his own. And now, there were two sets of dog prints instead of one.

"No! No!" he thought. "It's not true. I'm not following my own tracks. I'm not that stupid." But after following the tracks a few more feet, he conceded to reality: without the sun for reference and failing to check his compass, he had walked in a circle, then followed his own tracks around the circle a second time.

Spotting a nearby log, he sat down and planted his face on his hands; he was wounded and humiliated. How could he, Mittens, the skilled outdoorsman with a superb sense of direction, do something that stupid. He could only guess that his longing for human companionship caused and compounded the incident.

Millie looked up at him strangely as he suddenly began laughing. "Let's head back to camp," he chuckled. "I can't run fast enough to catch that fellow."

Staring intently at his compass, he left the circle and headed east until he reached Lake Isabella. After following the shoreline to his fish cache, he pulled out his supper and a couple extra to carry in the woods the next day. Later that night the fog lifted and the moon resumed its glow.

As he sat watching, his mind was still dwelling on the circle episode. "Why didn't I check my compass?" he thought. "Jack warned me about getting lost in fog. And, why did I circle to the left? Why does everybody circle to the left when they're lost? And why do track & field runners, horse racers and baseball players all circle to the left?" As his brain continued to spin around in left hand circles, he leaned back and drifted off to sleep.

* * * * *

At daybreak, he left the temporary camp and

followed the lake southwest until he reached the Isabella River. The current was too swift for the water to freeze as it bounced between the boulder strewn spillway and caused a thunderous roar as it poured out of the lake. Even in the cold of winter, the river had a rugged beauty. After crawling down the ice encrusted bank, he jumped from rock to rock until he had crossed, then continued his journey south.

An hour later, he reached the Island River. It was wide at that spot and after checking the ice thickness with his hatchet, he crossed to the other side. As the miles between him and the cabin increased, his confidence began to decrease. "Even if I get a deer," he thought. "How in the world will I drag it all the way back to the cabin?"

As he continued his relentless journey south — still not sighting deer tracks — his desperation grew. When he had hunted deer back in Hibbing, it was for sport. He was never overly concerned if he got one. The joy of being in the woods and taking a vacation was all he wanted. Now the situation was different. With the arrival of winter, fish and grouse were a scarce commodity and blueberries were extinct. He badly needed venison.

As he climbed to the top of a long flat topped ridge, he spotted a familiar sight in the snow: fresh deer tracks. He had to rub his eyes before he believed it, but there they were. The prints had large dew points and he guessed they were made by a buck or a big doe. "With tracks that big, it'll be easy to follow," he thought, as he started tracking.

Soon, the tracks led to a small clearing in a grove of jack pines where the deer had made a large scrape on the ground. The freshly pawed dirt told him that it was a buck in heat. He reasoned that it was probably a lone buck who had wandered into this deerless area looking for a mate. The buck had built the scrape to attract a doe and it meant one thing to Mittens: odds were strong that the buck would return to check the scrape.

Feeling that his best chance would be to sit and wait for the deer to return, he tossed together a makeshift deer stand. Selecting a boulder about 100 feet downwind of the scrape, he hefted a few logs onto it to use as a bench and piled branches next to it to break up his outline. To help keep warm on this breezy perch, he wrapped himself in a blanket. With his rifle at the ready, he waited...and waited...and waited. Nothing came. As the sun started sinking into the trees, he was getting chilly and decided to quit for the day. Thinking that the buck might visit the scrape early in the morning, he decided to set up camp for the night and return to the stand at dawn.

To avoid tainting the area with more human odor, he set up his camp several hundred yards from the stand. The camp wasn't as comfortable as the one he had built on Lake Isabella, but it was good enough for the one night that he planned to stay. Reaching in his pack, he pulled out a northern and fried it for supper. Concerned that frying fish in the morning could scare the deer away, he decided to eat the whole fish that night and skip breakfast.

It was still dark in the woods when he left camp the next morning. The moon had already set and he could barely see his tracks as he followed them back to the deer stand. The first small glimmer of light was appearing when he climbed onto the boulder. Concerned that he may have to sit for a long time in the cold, he unrolled his sleeping bag and wiggled inside. After wrapping the blanket around to form a tent and cuddling the dog next to him, he was ready to sit there all day if he had to.

Soon, the sun came up, but still no deer. After several hours, the only thing he had seen were a couple of ravens circling and a lumber jack bird begging for a handout. Even bundled as snuggly as he was, the cold relentless wind buffeting his face was beginning to get the best of him. But he would not and could not give up. The venison was too important.

As it neared mid-day, he started looking and feeling like a zombie. Unable to take the cold any longer, he decided to leave the stand for awhile and build a warm-up fire. Suddenly, he heard the distinctive "snap" of a twig breaking nearby. "No rabbit or squirrel is big enough to cause that sound," he thought. "It has to be a deer."

His pulse started to quicken as he gazed at the spot where the sound came from. Then he heard another twig snap. This one closer. Something was walking toward him. Slowly he removed his mittens, double checked his rifle, raised it to a shooting position and waited. As he sat in silence, he could hear a "thump-thump-thump" sound. Adrenalin was speeding through his body, causing his pulse to race. As tension built, he wasn't cold anymore.

After several nervous minutes, a branch near the cracking sound swayed slightly and he spotted part of a deer horn. A moment later, he saw the horn again and then it disappeared. The buck was stretching up to browse but still wasn't in view. Tense moments passed as he occasionally saw the horns and part of its face but the deer wouldn't step into the open clearing to give him a clear shot. After a few more moments, it stepped ahead a couple feet, exposing more of its head. Deciding to wait a little longer, he thought, "One more step. Just take one more step."

Suddenly a muffled "Grr-r-r-r" sound came from Millie; she had also spotted the buck. Quickly swinging his left hand down, he grabbed her mouth and held it shut. With one hand holding the dog's mouth and the other holding the gun, he was in an awkward position. The dog calmed down, but he couldn't risk taking his hand away from her mouth.

Finally the buck took a couple steps forward and presented a clear shot. "This is it", he thought, as he let go of the dog and put both hands on the rifle. With his pulse racing, he lined up the sights, took a deep breath and started to squeeze the trigger. Suddenly, "Woof - woof - woof," barked Millie. The buck leaped into the brush and was gone before Mittens could shoot.

"How could you do that?" he yelled. "Of all the times to bark, why did you pick this moment?" But Millie just looked up at him with her soft brown eyes, bewildered by the scolding he was giving. After several minutes, he started to cool down. After all, how could he blame the dog. She was only trying to protect her master from the vicious buck. "Besides," he thought. "Wasn't I the one who was questioning the intelligence of a hunter who takes his dog along on a deer hunt?"

Chapter 11

The Chase

After his nerves calmed and his wits returned, he thought about the situation. He felt the possibility of the buck returning to this spot was almost zero. The dog probably scared it into the next county and there was no sense in sitting in the stand any longer. Because he hadn't seen any other tracks, he speculated that this lone buck might be the only deer for miles around. Somehow, he had to find that same buck and try again.

He thought about a friend back in Hibbing who was a track star in school. The fellow used to brag that when there was good tracking snow, he could run down a deer. He claimed they were like a cheetah: the fastest thing in the forest during their initial burst of speed, but they quickly become exhausted and would have to stop and rest. While they were resting, he was still jogging and eventually he'd catch up. No one believed the guy, but the thought was intriguing. "What if he was telling the truth?" he thought. "As absurd as it sounds, could a man really outrun a deer in the woods?"

For starters, the person would have to be in great physical condition to sustain the pace. With his newly acquired, lean and muscular body — riding on legs of steel — Mittens felt a bit like a deer himself. The pursuit would require good tracking snow, which he had. It would take a lot of time, which he had. And, it would take someone who is so desperate for venison that he'd try almost anything. The description fit and he decided to go for it. After locating the tracks, he started following them in a slow jog.

The tracks took him over steep ridges, dense brush, and through some of the toughest swamps he had ever seen as he relentlessly followed them. Suddenly, the tracks were in a cluster. The deer had stopped to rest. Mittens began thinking that the track star was right. While the buck was resting, he was still moving. If so, he had narrowed the distance between himself and the deer. But he was beginning to tire and slowed to a fast walk. Although he was in great physical shape, he was carrying a heavy load. Slogging through foot deep snow while lugging a rifle and pack was starting to take a toll. "Maybe this isn't such a good idea after all," he thought.

Suddenly the pattern of the tracks changed. Instead

of being evenly spaced, the tracks were now in clusters every twenty feet — a sign that the deer was running. Besides himself, there were no other humans in the area and no wolves. He was the only one around who could cause the deer to panic and run. Suddenly, his hunting instincts kicked into gear; he was catching up.

Convinced he was closing the gap, he picked up the pace, moving as fast as he could while staying on the tracks. He held the pace as long as he could, but soon tired and had to rest. The deer was alternately running, walking and running again. Lacking the stamina to sustain a jogging pace, he went back to a fast walk, hoping the deer would get curious and stop. But the buck kept moving and stayed well ahead of him. He started to wonder if his friend had outrun a big fellow like this or just a small fawn.

As much as he hated to stop, darkness was coming and he had to give up the chase. He knew this would allow the buck to rest up and be fresh by morning, but he had no choice. Besides, he was worn out from the long chase and hungry from not eating all day. "Tomorrow, I'll have a full day, not a half day," he thought. "He won't get away this time."

It was too late in the day to build a comfortable camp; he had just enough daylight left to gather firewood for the evening campfire. Picking a spot by a large boulder, he threw down a few pine bows, stacked some firewood and got the fire started. With the overcast returning, darkness came quickly. He was exhausted from the chase and it felt great to sit down by the warmth of a fire and relax.

Reaching into his pack, he rooted around for the fish, but couldn't find it. He was sure he had placed two in the pack when he left the lake. He had eaten one the night before and there should have been one more left. It had either fallen out of the pack or he may have only put one in. "How stupid," he thought. "And to think that I passed up a couple grouse today because I thought I had another fish left. One day, I'm walking in circles, the next day I mess up with a deer, and now I've lost my supper. Maybe I've been in the woods too long. Or... maybe not long enough?"

Turning the pack upside down, he dumped everything on the ground. The only edibles he could find were a few leftover grouse bones that he had been saving for the dog. After heating up the frying pan, he threw in the bones and let them sizzle awhile. They smelled good, but chewing on them failed to ease his hunger. Even worse, the dog was whimpering and making him feel like a thief. Finally he gave up and tossed them to her.

Longing for something to eat, he briefly entertained the idea of walking back to the lake in the dark to get one of the fish. But common sense prevailed and he decided to tough it out through the night. Even if he didn't connect on a deer tomorrow, this time he'd remember to shoot a couple grouse. With his stomach growling, he curled up in his sleeping bag and listened

118

to the contented sound of Millie crunching on the bones. It made him wish he was a dog instead of a finicky human.

When morning came, he started a fire and made a pot of coffee. The coffee helped keep the walls of his stomach apart, but soon, he would have to find real food. He planned to resume tracking the deer the same as he did the day before, but as soon as a grouse or rabbit crossed his path, it would be lunch time.

After getting back on the deer tracks, the pursuit continued. Soon, he found a circle in the snow where the deer had bedded down for the night. A crust of ice had formed around the circle which meant that the deer had left hours earlier. There was a lot of catching up to do.

After an hour, the tracks changed from a walk to a trot and then a run. Although he was gaining, he was becoming concerned about the direction the deer was taking. The tracks kept heading south and if it continued, the buck would lead him all the way to Mexico. At the very least, he would be days away from camp — a week if he had to drag a deer back.

Finally the tracks turned west and followed a ridge. He began to notice a definite rhythm to the buck's running and resting and could almost predict when the deer would take its next break. Up ahead was a high ridge and he guessed that after climbing it, the deer would be resting on the other side. "This is my chance," he thought.

119

With a burst of speed, he climbed the ridge, then slowed to a crawl as he reached the top. Peeking over the edge, he carefully studied the thick wooded area for movement or a patch of brown. When he was sure nothing was there, he stood up and started down the hill. Suddenly, he heard a loud sneezing sound and the brush in front of him exploded as the buck escaped. Before he could shoulder his gun, the deer was out of sight except for a couple flashes of its white tail. He had caught the buck off guard, but didn't know until it was too late. Vowing not to repeat the mistake, he continued on.

A feeling of relief came as the buck changed course and headed north. He knew he had him now and it was only a matter of time before the deer zigged when it should have zagged and the further north it got before he converted it to venison, the less distance he'd have to drag it. After nearly outsmarting the deer, his level of confidence had ballooned. He was so certain he'd get the deer that he could already smell the venison frying in the pan.

The buck followed a series of northbound ridges and regularly crossed over to the adjoining ridge that paralleled it. Growing tired of the chase, Mittens decided to take a gamble: after the deer did another crossover, he would also cross, then cross again to the third ridge. Once there, he'd run until he was ahead of the buck, then stop and wait for it to come trotting through.

As he predicted, the tracks soon left the ridge, crossed the swampy area between ridges, then up onto the next one. With a grin on his face, he said, "I've got you now," and tore over to the third ridge. After running until he was far ahead, he stopped and waited. But the deer didn't come. After waiting several minutes, he went back to the other ridge and found that the tracks never wavered. The gamble failed and he had lost valuable time.

It was mid-day and he was hungry. Although he was keeping an eye out for small game, he hadn't seen anything all morning except a couple squirrels. It was almost two days since he had eaten and the grueling chase was sapping his strength. He had never gone this long without food and felt a gnawing in his stomach. With the buck heading north, the pursuit might take him to his fish cache on Lake Isabella or there was still a chance he'd spot a rabbit or grouse. With that hope in mind, he continued the pursuit.

Soon, the tracks changed to a run as he started closing the gap again. Topping a ridge, he caught another glimpse of the buck. Even if the deer stopped, it would have been out of range, but It gave him additional hope as he pressed on. Until now, he had frowned on the ways of the wolf. But with passion in his eyes and hunger clawing at his stomach, he began to feel like one of them.

Chapter 12

Going For Broke

Until now, the pursuit had followed the northbound ridges. However, when a different set of ridges intercepted at a right angle, the buck turned onto them and headed west. By now, It was mid afternoon and with no food, he had a big decision to make: if he gave up the chase and continued north, he'd eventually reach the Isabella River. Even in the dark, he could follow the river to the lake where he had food cached. But the next day it would take so long to get back to the deer tracks that drifting snow could make the tracks impossible to follow. The buck would be gone for good with no guarantee of finding another. But if he continued the pursuit heading west and failed to get the deer, he would be in for a long, miserable and hungry night.

And, he couldn't be sure that he'd find food the following day. Heading west could place him in serious jeopardy.

After pondering the choices, he decided to continue the pursuit. He simply had to have that buck and didn't care what the price of failure was. The answer was easy: don't fail. With a determination he hadn't felt before, he started following the tracks west.

Again, he caught a glimpse of the buck fleeing, but it was too far away. As he picked up the pace and began jogging, the intervals between the buck walking, trotting and running got smaller. Again, he spotted the buck on a nearby ridge, this time it was closer than it had been all day. It was becoming clear that the buck was either tiring or becoming annoyed. The deer wasn't the only one tiring. Stopping to catch his breath, he could hear his heart pounding wildly. "I'm too young to have a heart attack," he declared, as he resumed the pace. Soon, he was catching a glimpse of the buck every 10 minutes, but never long enough to get a clear shot.

As the chase continued, the sun was getting close to the trees and darkness began closing in. Mittens said, "This is it! It's now or never." Removing the heavy pack and dropping it on the ground, he broke into a run. As he smashed through the brush and narrowed the distance between himself and the deer, he could hear brush crashing ahead of him as the buck bounded through the woods.

Pushing back the limits of his endurance, he

struggled for breath and clutched his aching sides as he ran. He desperately wanted to stop and rest, but knew that all the effort would be in vain if he quit now. Even though the buck showed no signs of quitting, he relentlessly kept up the pursuit. As the forest grew darker, he knew that in a few minutes, he'd have no choice but to quit.

Suddenly, he broke into a small clearing and to his shock, the buck was standing there facing him — 30 feet away — ready to do battle. Its head was down low, steam poured from its nostrils and the wild look on its face seemed to say: "Come and get me!" Mittens panicked and froze in his tracks.

The buck started pawing the ground as if it was preparing to charge. Mittens raised the gun, but was breathing so heavily from the run that he couldn't hold it steady. As he yanked the trigger the gun went off and he could see the sights head for the ground. Untouched, the buck dived into the brush and disappeared.

The reality of what happened sunk in quickly and he yelled. "No! You can't do it. You're not getting away." Mustering all his strength, he tore off into the brush in hot pursuit. After only a hundred yards, the buck stopped again and faced him at close range. "This is crazy," he thought. "Is that deer trying to commit suicide?"

Again, he raised the rifle. And again, he started shaking and trembling. After taking several deep breaths and a long pause, he squeezed the trigger as carefully as he could. The gun fired and the buck fell. Mittens stood in stunned silence for a moment, then in a state of total exhaustion, collapsed on top of the deer and went to sleep.

THE CELEBRATION

It was pitch dark when he awoke to the wetness of Millie licking his face. He didn't know how long he was out, but his sweat drenched clothing was getting crunchy from the cold. "We did it girl! We did it!" he said as he hugged the dog. "Tonight, we're going to party. We're having a feast."

After looking around for the pack, he remembered he had dropped it several ridges back while chasing the deer. Even in darkness, the snow gave a pale glow — enough that he could faintly see his tracks. After tracing them for a few hundred yards, they crossed a rocky area and faded. The wind was picking up speed and whipping the snow around, covering the tracks.

After a bit of searching, he picked up the trail again, followed it to the next ridge and lost it again. It was becoming more than an annoying problem. Finding the pack in daylight would be a breeze, but he couldn't wait until morning. Matches for lighting a fire and the knife for processing the deer were in the pack. It made him shudder to think of spending a night without fire sitting next to a mountain of food that he couldn't eat.

As he walked to the next ridge, hoping to find the tracks, he heard a noise behind him: Millie was barking at something." Shut up," he yelled. "Can't you see I've got enough trouble?" But the barking continued, so he turned around and walked over to see what the noise was all about. When he got to the dog, she was panting and wagging her tail while she sat...next to the pack. In the darkness, he had walked right past it. Patting the dog on the head, he said, "Maybe you'll make a good deer hunter after all."

After walking back to the buck and stumbling around in the darkness collecting wood, he got a fire going. As the flames lit up the surroundings, he took a closer look at the deer. It was bigger than he had thought: five tines on each horn and he guessed that it weighed over 200 pounds. "How in the world will I drag that monster all the way back to the cabin?" he thought. It was a problem — a lovely problem — that he'd deal with in the morning. Right now, he was hungry.

Just minutes after field dressing the deer, he was roasting a piece of tenderloin on the open fire while Millie sat chewing on a bone. He liked meat well done, but at this moment, rare would do just fine. As he chomped into the sweet taste of the tenderloin, he couldn't remember anything tasting so good. Maybe his state of hunger had something to do with it, but at that moment, the taste of venison was rivaling Louise's blueberry pie.

Later that night, the overcast that had lingered for so long finally lifted and the moon lit up the campsite. As he sat there with Millie's head resting on his lap, he thought about the choice he had made earlier that day: head for the safety and food of the other camp, or gamble that he'd get the deer.

Again, he had gambled and won. Although, he didn't care to dwell on the consequences of losing, he didn't lose and he was proud. Proud that he had achieved something that few others would even dream of attempting. He had outrun a mature buck on its home turf. Or, should he say that he "annoyed" it into submission? It didn't matter. Just like his friend, the track star, no one would believe the story anyway. But even though he performed the feat to an audience of none, he felt the same elation that a ball player would feel after hitting a home run in the World Series.

Chapter 13

The Long Way Home

As the morning sun appeared, he crawled slowly out of his sleeping bag — stiff and sore from the long chase. After stoking up the fire and making coffee, he fried a piece of venison while he studied the map. He only had a vague idea of where he was, and for all he knew, he could be completely off the map. The only thing certain was that if he headed north, eventually he'd reach the Isabella River. To limit the deer dragging distance, he chose a northeast compass course.

After rigging his pack, he grabbed the buck by the horns and started pulling. Scooting downhill, the dragging was easy. But it quickly got tough when the rugged terrain went uphill. Throwing a rope around the horns, he tied it around his waist and leaned ahead.

Grunting and groaning, he inched his way up the hill.

The hours dragged on and still no sign of familiar territory. He thought about leaving the deer behind and walking ahead to insure that he was on the correct course, but he worried that if he left the deer alone, wolves might get it. As hard as he had worked to get it, he wasn't going to risk losing it.

After a few more hours of dragging, he topped a ridge and far below he could see the Isabella River. It was late in the day, so he set up camp in a grove of trees on top of the ridge. He and Millie had a huge serving of venison that night. "The more of it we eat, the easier it will be to drag," he joked.

The next morning, he pulled the deer to the river, checked the thickness of the ice and crossed. Following the river, he reached Rice Lake and soon was in the area where he had gotten lost in the overcast and walked in a circle. Determined not to repeat the mistake, he carefully took an east compass heading.

Late in the day, he arrived triumphantly at his temporary camp by Lake Isabella. There was no band playing or "Welcome Home" flags fluttering. Just a couple of lumberjack birds trying to scavenge leftover crumbs. With the camp already built and an hour or two of daylight left, he grabbed his fishing tackle and headed for his hot spot on the bay. But it was a waste of time; nothing was biting. The moon over the campsite wasn't as bright as it was before, but the uncomfortable feeling of not having a deer was gone. Happy to be back in familiar territory, he slept well that night.

After breakfast, he went out on the lake for one last try at the northerns. It didn't take long and he landed a nice ten pounder. He wanted to stick around and try for a few more, but he was becoming concerned about the weight in his already overweight pack. Deciding to leave, he gathered his tackle, picked up the remaining fish in his cache and left the lake.

Back at camp, he stuffed the rest of his gear into the pack, then tossed in the extra fish. "Holy Cow!" he thought, as he hoisted the pack onto his shoulders. "Dragging a deer and carrying this is gonna be too much. There's got to be a better way." Removing the fish and a couple other items from the pack, he banded them tightly together with rope and tied the end in a loop which he hooked to Millie's collar. She looked at him as if to say, "You're joking!"

Tossing the pack on his back, he grabbed the deer and started dragging while he yelled at the dog, "C'mon you huskies. Mush!" After towing it 50 feet, the fish pack wound around a bush and the dog came to a halt. Walking back, he untangled the rope, shortened it and tried again. Another 50 feet went by and the dog tangled her front leg in the rope, tripped and started howling.

"Well, it was a good try," he thought, as he untied the rope, stuffed the fish inside the deer's body cavity and resumed dragging. With the deer heavier and the brush thicker, every obstacle brought him to a halt. But the biggest problem was the horns snagging on the brush. The day before, when the deer was lighter, he could easily yank it free. With the added weight, it was now a lot tougher.

Sizing up the deer, he tried to decide if there were any parts he could discard. The hide was needed to protect the carcass during dragging and the legs would make good dog food. That left only the horns. Removing them would shave only a small amount of weight, but would eliminate the brush hang-ups. He dearly wanted to keep them as a souvenir, but decided the meat was more important than a trophy. Gritting his teeth, he pulled out his axe, cut off the horns and carried them to the lake. With a small piece of rope, he tied them to a tree so he could find them later.

Walking to the edge of the high bank overlooking the lake, he took one last look. A cold wind was chilling his cheeks and peppering his face with flakes of snow as he stared at Isabella's bleak expanse of ice and snow. As he stood there shivering, he told himself that someday he'd return. Maybe he'd be back in a few weeks to go fishing and retrieve his deer horns. Or, maybe he'd come back in summer. He could paddle up the Isabella River to get there and then he would see how the lake looked when it was cloaked in green with the water blue instead of white. "Yes, someday I'll be back." he promised. But like the promise to Louise, it was another one he would not keep.

Chapter 14

Return Of The Wolf

It was an all day hike from his cabin to the lake, so he planned for two days of deer dragging to get back. Taking a northerly route, he stayed in the lowlands, avoiding ridges. Removing the horns made the dragging easier and by nightfall, he was beyond the halfway point and setting up camp. "Tomorrow night, we'll be sitting in our warm cabin," he said to Millie as he roasted another steak on the fire.

Up before daylight, he continued north and by midday he reached the Ahmoo Creek and his fantasy spot by the twin waterfalls. After climbing onto his favorite boulder, he reached in the pack and pulled out Millie's ball. Giving it a hard throw, it disappeared in the snow, close to the creek. Like magic, she found it right away and brought it back. Giving it another fling, he wondered how the dog could cover so many miles in the woods and still have energy left to chase a ball.

After leaving the creek, a warm feeling came over him as he dragged the deer up the final ridge and saw his cabin below. It was becoming his home and after a week away, it was good to be back. Checking out the camp, he found everything still in its place. After dusting the snow off the door, he entered the cabin, took out a pencil and X-ed off the days on the calendar that he was gone.

By his estimate, it was the 1st of December and in a month he would leave. Even though living off the land was tough and he missed being around people, the thought of leaving the wilderness made him sad. In spite of the hardships, he had a lot of fun building the cabin and he enjoyed hunting, fishing and working the trapline. But he was taking a lot of risks and with every new gamble, an inner voice told him he didn't belong here and it was time to leave. Yet another voice — intoxicated by the mystical waters and the sweet smelling fragrance of pines — begged him to stay.

He was tired and needed a break from the long hunting ordeal but first he had to take care of the deer. Working by firelight, he wrestled the frozen hide off and quartered the carcass. The next morning, he cut it into 36 portions — one for every day in December, and a few for emergency. Of course, he'd have other food besides venison, but to be on the safe side, he rationed

134

it to make sure it would last until the end of the month.

After packing the fish and venison away and cutting a stack of firewood, he took a break and loafed around camp the rest of the day. After supper, he remembered it was his birthday. He was turning 22 which was cause for a celebration. After rummaging through his gear, he found an old hunk of chocolate that he'd saved for a special occasion. He had trapped a lot of fur, bagged a deer and survived in the wilderness for several months. Certainly that accomplishment also qualified as a special occasion. Biting into the old frozen chunk of chocolate, he twisted his face, trying to find the taste. Soon it melted in his mouth. It was delicious.

He almost wished he hadn't opened the delicacy. Sampling this piece of civilization could ruin his taste for fish and venison. As he chewed on the chocolate, Millie looked up at him with those soft brown eyes and started whining. Mittens' heart melted like the chocolate. How could he forget his old friend. "Don't you know that chocolate's bad for dogs?" he said, as he patted her on the head. But the dog seemed to know that she could get anything she wanted from him by using those sad eyes. Giving in, he broke off a chunk and tossed it to her. She didn't believe in savoring treats and downed it in one gulp.

The birthday party wasn't over yet; He still had to break out the booze. Along with the other supplies, Jack had tossed in a couple bottles of home brew that a friend made. "They're for medicinal use," he had joked.

Mittens didn't care too much for booze, but he figured that since he hauled the bottles all the way out there, at least he should sample one.

After popping the cork, he poured some in his cup and took a swallow. Suddenly his mouth felt like it was on fire. With a blast, he blew it out then rinsed his mouth with water. The bottle contained clear moonshine — over 100 proof. Jack said it was good stuff, but to Mittens, it tasted like gasoline. "I'd have to be terminally ill to use this for medicinal purposes," he mumbled as he corked the bottle and shoved it back into the rafters.

* * * * * *

With the hunting trip over, it was back to work. The first task was resetting traps on the east route near Arrow Lake. Halfway through the job, he decided to give the lake one more try for northerns. If he could catch a few more fish, it would add variety to the venison. His hot spot on the bog had changed to a dead hole, so he decided to fish away from shore. The ice was several inches thick and tough to chop, but he got a hole dug and tossed in a line. After trying almost everything he had, he couldn't get a nibble. Late in the day, he gave up in disgust. "It's a good thing I like venison," he thought. "I wonder if I'll still enjoy it at the end of the month?"

The next day, he started re-setting traps in earnest. Or, at least he tried. The colder temperature and added snow on the ground made the sets tough to rebuild. When working around water, his sensitive hands got so cold that he had to stop often and build a fire to thaw out. At the rate he was going, he'd have to reduce the line to a single circle route.

Along with the increased snow and cold, he had another new problem: wolf tracks. He thought the wolves had left, but they were back in the area. He considered carrying a rifle when working the line, but the need to carry a gun still hadn't sunk in and he felt

he'd be OK without it. After all, the wolves were minding their own business and leaving him alone. If they started bothering him again, he could always start carrying a gun.

After re-building trap sets all day and half of the next, he completed the Arrow Lake sets and started working his way west. As he followed the trail around the big hill by the south end of the lake, Millie started growling. "What's the matter, girl?" he said. Suddenly, she took off running up the hill. "I hope it's not another porcupine," he laughed. But the laugh changed to a look of terror as he glanced up at the hill. The black and gray wolf were standing side by side in a clearing near the top and the dog was running straight towards them.

Throwing down his pack, he charged up the hill, yelling at her to come back. But the dog was determined to drive the wolves away and couldn't be stopped. By the time he got halfway up the hill, she had already reached the wolves and tore into them. The two wolves held their ground and fought back. While the forest screamed with the awful sound of animals fighting, Mittens scrambled up the hill as fast as he could. When he got within 100 feet of the fight, he let out a yell and the wolves dashed into the woods. Millie was lying in the snow, covered in blood. She was no match for the wolves who had ripped her from limb to limb. As she lay in the snow whimpering, he sat down, gently picked her up and cradled her in his arms.

"Why didn't you stop when I yelled?" he scolded.

138

"Maybe now you'll start listening to me." The whimpering continued while he tried to comfort her. "I'll get you back to the cabin and patch you up," he said. "In a few weeks, you'll be as good as new and we'll be playing fetch with your ball again." But it was not to be. Millie stopped whimpering, raised her head and looked at Mittens as if she was saying, "So long old partner." Then as her head slowly lowered onto his arms, her soft brown eyes closed forever.

He hadn't cried since he was in grade school, but now the tears streamed down his cheeks. She was just a dog, a half breed at that, but she was the only true friend he had. "How can this beautiful place take her away?" he cried. "How can this place that I love so much, become so cruel and wretched? It's not right. It's not fair."

Sitting in silence on the hillside, he continued blaming the forest and the wolves, refusing to concede that one shot in the air with a gun would have sent the wolves running — if he had been carrying a gun. But no matter how great his remorse, he knew that sorrow would never heal her wounds and tears could never turn back the hands of time. Life would have to go on without her.

After an hour, he cut a pair of spruce poles, tied the dog to them and towed her to their favorite spot by the Ahmoo Creek: the place where she loved to fetch the ball; the place where she tangled with the porcupine and the place where he'd often go to see the sun go

139

down and the watch the waters flow past the teetering rocks.

After placing her on a spot by the creek, he covered her with stones. "The wolves won't bother you anymore," he said. Then he climbed up on his favorite boulder, high above the creek, and watched the sun go down. The red, yellow and gold clouds lit the trees in a blaze of color — as if to honor his fallen friend. Reaching into his pack, he pulled out her ragged ball. Clutching it in his hands, he looked sadly at the battered threads and teeth marks. Then he stood up and threw the ball as hard as he could. "Go get it girl," he yelled.

Chapter 15

Vengeance

He had grown so used to having Millie around that he felt lost without her. Her vacant spot in the corner left an emptiness that made the cabin seem cold and gloomy. When he walked the trapline, he missed hearing the familiar sound of her footsteps behind him. All he could hear now was the ghostly silence of the forest. To fight the loneliness, he immersed himself in the job at hand and tried to forget his problems. But his problems were only beginning. The wolves were still in the area.

Killing his dog wasn't enough. Now, they were stalking the trapline and stealing his catch. Although there may have been more, he felt there were only two wolves causing problems: the female gray which he now called "Gray Ghost" and the black male he called "Devil Eyes".

His hatred of them had grown so strong that it clouded his thinking. His thoughts turned to revenge and his trap sets changed from beaver to wolf as he vowed to avenge Millie's death. But the wolves were smarter than he thought. They eluded his traps and seemed to know when he was carrying a rifle and what it would do. They liked to sneak around the woods — sometimes in plain sight — as if they were taunting him. But if he had a gun, they wouldn't stick around long enough for him to get a shot. It became clear that his best chance of getting them would be to sharpen his trapping skills.

After snaring some rabbits, he decided to try a few of Jack's "can't fail" wolf sets. After locating an open clearing with large rocks, he placed a rabbit on one of the rocks. When it's winter in the North Woods, there's no free lunch, and wolves know that. They won't simply walk up to the rock and take the rabbit bait. They'll circle the rock several times, trying to figure out what's wrong. That's how he was going to outwit them. Instead of placing traps by the bait, he placed them around the rock — away from the bait. Jack told him that when the wolf circles the rock, it will step into one of the traps. Working all day, he built six of the sets, all carefully camouflaged to hide human odor.

The next morning, he could barely contain his excitement as he went out to check the traps. He was

142

confident that by the end of the day, he'd have wolf hides hanging by the cabin. But the confidence melted when he arrived at the first set: every trap was sprung and the bait was gone. He was dumbfounded and wondered, "How did they do that?"

After picking up the traps, he hiked to the next set and found the same scene — traps sprung and the bait gone. They were following his tracks to each set and getting a free meal at his expense. At the final set, they paid for the food with the ultimate insult: leaving a pile of wolf scat where the bait was. They were doing more than outsmarting him. They were making a fool of him.

Back at the cabin, he was fuming. He had tried every trick he knew to catch them, but they were too clever. But he had one more idea floating around in his vengeance filled brain. He decided that the next day he would fire the ultimate weapon at them: run them down. The idea sounded stupid, but the idea of running down a deer also sounded stupid — until he tried it. He would leave the pack at the cabin and carry only the rifle and bare essentials to give him extra speed. He didn't expect to actually outrun them. But with his legs of steel, he would get on their track, pursue them at a fast pace and annoy the tar out of them in the hope that they'd stop and challenge him — like the buck did.

He had a spring in his step as he left the cabin the next day. Without the heavy pack, he was taking long strides with ease as he headed down the trail to the spot where he had placed his first wolf set. He guessed that the wolves would return to that place, looking for another free meal. He was right; The fresh tracks meant they had returned and were close by.

He took off after them at a fast pace, following the fresh tracks. The wind was in his favor and the soft snow muffled his footsteps as he hurried towards them. As he topped a hill, he spotted them down below, laying next to a pine tree. He had caught them napping. Quickly tossing the gun to his shoulder, he cocked the hammer, but they were too quick. Before he could get one in his sights, they disappeared into the timber.

Because he had alerted them to his presence, he no longer had to be cautious and quiet, so he tore off into the timber in hot pursuit. After following their tracks up and over several ridges, he started getting tired and stopped to rest. He felt he would have to establish a non-stop, relentless pursuit to stay with them. This meant changing to a fast walk and running only when a hill was ahead that presented an opportunity to surprise them.

The chase continued for hours. Gradually, the wolves made a large circle to the south, returned to the same place where the pursuit began, then cut through a small open meadow. When Mittens reached the meadow, he stopped. It contained hundreds of wolf tracks and he couldn't figure out which sets were the correct ones to follow. The meadow was a place where the wolves regularly looked for mice and it was blanketed with their tracks.

144

After wasting an hour circling the perimeter of the meadow to determine which set of tracks were the correct ones leaving the meadow, he resumed the chase. This time, the wolves made a large circle to the west and after a couple hours, returned to the same track infested meadow. He had wasted a whole day and they had made a fool of him again.

That night, he had another new plan: Since they liked that meadow so much, he decided to build a stand on the side of it and hide there. When they walked in, he'd nail them. It was a fool-proof plan and without Millie around to bark, he'd get them for sure.

The next morning, he was building a stand at the clearing. Picking the downwind side, he piled brush on top of a boulder and sat down to wait. After a few hours, he got cold and went back to the cabin to warm up. An hour later, he was back on the stand, patiently waiting. Several more hours passed and he was cold again. His idea was another dud and it was time to try something different. Suddenly, he felt that cold clammy feeling again. The same feeling he felt before when he thought someone was watching him. He slowly turned his head to the right, then left, but saw nothing. There was nothing behind him, nothing ahead. "Why do I have that uncomfortable feeling," he thought.

Shifting his body around, he stared into the timber directly behind him. Suddenly, he saw it: Devil Eyes was watching him. His black fur blended in with the darkness of the dense spruce, but he couldn't hide those

145

satanic eyes. Slowly and carefully, Mittens brought the rifle up to his shoulder, but as soon as he lined up the sights, the wolf was gone. Leaping off the boulder, he ran to the spot where Devil Eyes stood. Picking up the tracks, he tore off after the wolf, hurdling deadfalls, smashing through the brush and chasing the wolf through the woods with reckless abandon. But it was another hopeless cause; the wolf was too quick, too smart, too cunning and Mittens was too slow — physically and mentally.

The chase led to the Ahmoo Creek and the place where he had buried Millie a week earlier. Out of breath and out of ambition, he decided to climb up onto his favorite boulder and take a break. The boulder was becoming more than a scenic place to sit. It was also a place where he could think. When he sat up high on this perch and surveyed the sights around him, his clouded mind always seemed to clear.

As he sat there, catching his breath, he started to wonder, "Why! Why am I doing this? Why am I making a monkey out of myself chasing these wolves around the woods? After wasting a whole week trying to get revenge, I haven't come close and probably never will. I'm tired of this place. I hate the wolves, I hate the snow and the cold and I'm sick of eating venison every single day. I want to leave."

He still had three weeks to stay and couldn't resume his trapline. Not with the wolves robbing his traps. It would take nearly a week to haul the furs and gear back

146

to Insula Lake which left two weeks. If he left now, he could take his time hauling stuff back, build a good lean-to at the lake and hunt and fish until Jack arrived. The temporary camp wouldn't be as comfortable as the cabin, but he felt he couldn't stay in the area any longer. He decided to head back to the cabin and start packing.

As he started to stand up, his foot slipped on the icy surface and sent him sprawling face down onto the hard boulder. When he tried to get back on his feet, he slipped again and started slowly sliding toward the steep edge that faced the creek. Unable to stop, he grabbed a small bush that was growing out of a crack in the boulder and hung on as he slid over the edge. Dangling above the creek, he quickly found a small ledge to place his feet, then tried to climb back up.

As hard as he tried, he couldn't get a grip to pull himself back onto the boulder. Hanging there precariously, he looked down at the cold, icy water. If he let go, it would only be about a five foot fall, but there were some nasty looking rocks to land on. Struggling hard, he again tried to climb, but there was too much ice to get a grip.

As he eyed the creek below, he noticed a large gap between two rocks. If he could land between those rocks, it would be no problem. But if he missed, he'd walk away with some nasty bruises. He might even sprain an ankle. Confident that he'd land in the open spot, he lowered himself as far as he could, pushed away from the face of the boulder, and jumped.

147

Chapter 16

The Fallen Warrior

As he dropped into the rocky creek, his right hip smacked into one of the teetering rocks, spun him around and sent him sprawling part way into the icy water — almost sending him over the falls. As he started to crawl out of the creek, he cursed the rocks. "Dang! Now I wish a tourist would have rolled those rocks over the falls. A guy could get hurt with those things sitting there," he joked. But the rocks were no joke. As he started to get up, he felt a sharp pain in the upper part of his right leg. "Ouch! I think I bruised my leg when I hit that rock," he mumbled.

As he hobbled away from the creek, the leg felt weak and gimpy, but it only hurt when he put his weight on it. Concerned that he may have sprained it, he cut down a small sapling and made a makeshift crutch to help keep the weight off. As he limped toward the cabin, he grew more concerned about the condition of the leg. "If it's sprained bad enough, I may have to stay in the cabin another week before packing out," he groaned.

When he arrived at the cabin, the pain was worse. Simply touching his right leg to the ground felt like a bolt of lightning shooting through his body. Gritting his teeth, he crawled inside the cabin and got the stove started. After removing his clothing, he stared at the leg in disbelief; the upper femur bone was broken, close to the hip. A large lump was pushing up — almost breaking through the skin — and the leg was turned at an impossible angle.

He didn't need a medical degree to understand how serious the situation was. This type of break — difficult to splint or cast — demanded specialized medical care. Alone in the wilderness with no one to help, he was in big trouble. There was no other choice than to build a cast and attempt to reset the bone himself.

Sliding on his rump, he pulled himself out to the woodpile and brought back several sticks of pine. Because the break was well above his knee, the cast would have to go up to the hip. While he whittled away on the wood sticks, making a cast, the area around the break continued to swell and the pain increased. After wrapping the leg with a piece of blanket, he placed five of the sticks vertically around the break and looped it with pieces of rope to hold the sticks in place. Tightening

150

the ropes would lock the leg firmly in place, but first he had to straighten the break. As he pressed his hand lightly on the broken area, the pain overwhelmed him and the cabin echoed with his screams.

After a few moments, the pain subsided and he thought about the moonshine Jack had sent along for "medicinal purposes". Reaching into the rafters, he pulled the bottle down and yanked the cork off. To his surprise, when he took a gulp of the evil liquid, it went straight down and stayed there. The pain in his leg was so intense that he could barely feel the bite of the moonshine.

After a few more gulps, the room started spinning around and the pain seemed to go away. The medicine was doing its stuff, so he decided to give the leg straightening another try. It occurred to him that after he pushed the bone straight, he'd have to quickly tighten and knot the rope to lock it in place. If the pain was too intense, he might not be able to tie the knot and the bone would spring back crooked. He decided to tie a slip hitch into one of the ropes so it would lock when pulled. His plan was to hold the rope with his left hand, then using his right hand, push the leg into position and give the rope a yank. Holding the rope — ready to pull — he placed his hand on the break, took a deep breath and pushed down as hard as he could.

While screaming in pain, he pushed harder, but the break wouldn't move. Unable to stand it any longer, he stopped pushing. The intense pain throbbed for

151

several minutes, then finally subsided. With trembling hands, he grabbed the bottle of moonshine and took a few more swallows. It was now going down like drinking water while his brain fought to stay in focus. Sitting there in a drunken stupor, the intense pain was the only thing keeping him awake. That, and the fear of leaving the leg the way it was. If he allowed it to heal in a bent position, he would be crippled for life. He dreaded the thought of touching the break again, but knew that somehow, he had to straighten it.

His head stopped spinning and his thoughts came into focus. If he could figure a way to use counter-traction to tug on his ankle and stretch the leg, the break would bend easier. And if he built a lever that would give him a mechanical advantage, he would have more bending power. Grabbing his knife, he started whittling on a stick. Soon he had fashioned a long lever device with a rocking point notched around another stick. The lever would have far more force than he could muster with his bare hand and, hopefully, enough to do the job.

Looping a rope around the ankle of the broken leg, he tossed the end of the rope over one of the rafters, sat on a chair and held the rope. He planned to knock the chair away and his falling body weight would tighten the rope and stretch the leg. It would require perfect timing to slam the lever down, straighten the break and tighten the slip hitch knot while his body briefly dangled from the rafters.

152

With the slip hitch and traction rope in his left hand and the lever in his right, he lowered the lever gently against the break. Lightly touching it caused him to scream in pain. "I can't do it! I can't do it!" he cried, as he let go of the lever, grabbed the bottle and took another gulp.

His brain was becoming so scrambled that even sitting on a chair, he had trouble maintaining his balance. Finally he yelled, "I am Charles 'Mittens' Perkins, the toughest man in the woods. I can take the pain." As he pushed the chair away, he slammed the lever down on his leg as hard as he could. The bone popped into alignment and with a scream and a yank of the hitch rope, he locked the splint into place, released the other rope and fell to the floor.

The cabin walls shook from the sound of his blood curdling screams as the pain increased for several minutes. When it started to ease, he bound the splint with several more ropes — locking it firmly in place. As his body started shaking and shivering from the shock, he loaded the stove with so much wood that the cabin heated up like a sauna. Then, rolling onto the bed, he heaped blankets and hides on his trembling body and when the pain finally eased, he slowly went to sleep.

A NEW DAY DAWNING

Sunshine was peeking through the tiny window of the cabin when he finally awoke. His first thought was "I'm alive!" The pain in his leg was almost gone and the terrible experience of setting the break seemed like a long time ago. So long that he began to wonder just how long he had slept. Was it only for a night or was it more than a day. His stomach answered the question for him. He was hungry. Very hungry.

Wiggling out of bed and onto the floor, he dragged himself outside to get venison and firewood. After curing his hunger, he looked around the cabin and saw the bottle of moonshine still lying on the floor. It was over half gone and he couldn't believe he drank that much. Uncorking the bottle, he took a swallow. As his mouth turned to fire and he quickly spit it out, he declared, "Yep, I'm going to be OK."

Concerned about his leg, he carefully cut and peeled back a chunk of the blanket that covered the broken area. The skin was turning black and the swelling was pushing the skin tightly against the sticks. He could wiggle his foot and his toes were working fine, but he worried about the dark color of the skin. " Could this be gangrene?" he thought. "Am I going to die?"

He had little knowledge of medicine, but felt quite proud of the job he had done. "Could anyone else have built a cast from pine limbs and set their own broken leg?" he thought. He had experienced a few failures on the trip, but he had also faced a few tough challenges and came out on top. But now, he faced an even greater challenge. The biggest of his life: getting out of the woods alive.

Chapter 17

A Change Of Plan

Glancing at the calendar, he noticed it was marked to December 7, the day he went to the clearing and later had the accident. He marked off one more day, but thinking he could be off a few days, questioned the accuracy. To get maximum healing time, he planned to wait until the last possible day before leaving for Lake Insula. Calendar correctness was becoming a factor.

He didn't look forward to sitting in the cabin that long, but he had a big stack of firewood outside the door and a locker full of venison. Assuming he didn't get ill from the broken leg, he could survive comfortably. During the wait, he could whittle out a good set of crutches and when the three weeks were up, he'd limp over to the lake and have Jack carry the furs and gear out.

Sitting in a tiny cabin was no picnic and the days dragged slowly by. On sunny days, he crawled outside and sat for hours staring at the swamp. The big thrill of the day occurred in the morning when he got to mark another day off the calendar. After several days, the swelling in the leg started going down, skin color was returning and the healing proceeded nicely. He questioned if three weeks of healing would be enough, but someone once told him that bones heal fast when you're young. "I hope they're right," he declared. "Because, even if I have to crawl, I'll be at that lake on New Years."

As the days dragged on, the wood pile dwindled. Before the broken leg, he had cleaned up all the wood close to camp and had to forage deep into the woods to get the pile. He decided to bundle up a bit tighter and run the stove only for cooking. He still had plenty of venison. So much, he was getting tired of it. And, with Millie gone, there was even more to go around. It was a good diet for healing a broken leg, but he dreamed of eating a bowl of blueberries or a piece of Louise's pie.

"The first thing I'll do when I get back to Winton is go to the cafe and order everything on the menu," he mused. "If Louise is there and has blueberry pie, I won't eat just a slice. I'll eat the whole pie."

As the word "Louise" entered his brain, sweet thoughts came out the other side. He promised he'd be

156

back to see her, and while staying at Jack's he had plenty of chances to do it. But he invented a thousand reasons not to and now he started to wonder if he made a mistake. "If I can fall in love with a dog — even a boulder," he thought, "How can I be sure that she can't fall for a jobless, penniless, overweight person like me?" But as he thought about it more, he remembered that the boulder he loved, broke his leg and the dog he loved, broke his heart. Fearing she would do the same, he struggled to erase her memory.

As New Years approached, he started becoming upbeat. The soreness in his leg was completely gone and the color had returned to normal. It was rough to stare at the cabin walls every day, but soon the place would be only a memory. Whether he'd someday look fondly on the experience was a point of debate. If he could get over losing Millie and not have a limp from the broken leg, he'd likely remember only the good times.

When Christmas arrived, he again questioned the calendar's accuracy. Besides the possible error when he broke his leg, there were a few days during the fall when he wasn't certain he had marked the day. For all he knew, year end might be a day or two away instead of a week and dragging a bum leg for two miles through the woods could take several days. If the calendar was correct, he'd have to wait at the lake a few extra days, but the change of scenery would be a blessing. With cabin fever corroding his brain, and visions of blueberry pie gnawing at his stomach, he decided to leave the next day.

When morning came. he started to pack. After packing his sleeping bag, axe, knife and other essentials, he stuffed in enough venison to last a week in case he arrived too early. He'd have to leave a small amount of food behind, but Jack would be visiting the cabin while retrieving the other gear and he would need food. And, he'd be happy to find the left-over moonshine.

One last essential he stuffed into the pack was the rifle. He still had a score to settle with the wolves and if he saw one, he wanted to be ready. After tightening the leg cast, he hobbled out of the cabin. The snow had become deeper in the last few weeks and was now up to his knees. Rolling onto his back, he slithered up onto the rock ledge by the cabin and slowly got back on his feet.

The sun was bright, almost blinding, as he stood on the ledge overlooking the cabin and swamp. Taking one last look , he felt a bit lonesome — like he was leaving an old friend. "Will I ever return?" he thought. "Well, maybe." Then, he took another look, shook his head and thought, "No, that cabin is a torture chamber. I don't want to see it again. Ever!"

ONE MORE TIME

To keep the weight off his leg, he decided to drag the pack behind him with a rope tied to his waist. Balancing on his crutches, he kicked away the snow in front of him and as he swung forward, his crutches became tangled in the alder bushes. After untangling the crutches and kicking away more snow, he tried again. This time, the pack rope tightened in mid-swing and he almost lost his balance.

He attached more rope, then stopped every twenty feet to pull the pack up to him. This worked a bit better but progress was still slow. After a half hour, he had traveled only 100 yards from the cabin. With two miles of dense forest ahead, he could see that it might take more than a couple days to reach the lake. But he was in no hurry. "If I'm late, Jack will wait," he thought, as he continued hobbling through the brush.

Soon he approached a small clearing. "Aha!" he thought. "Easy going up ahead." But there was a reason the brush wasn't growing in that spot. He couldn't see that the snow was hiding a three foot deep crevice in the rocky ground, and as he swung ahead, he dropped into the hidden trap. His left leg went in cleanly, but the cast on the right leg jammed against the rocks. As he crashed down on the bad leg, he heard a loud "snap".

When he stood upright, stuck in the crevice, a sharp pain was hammering his bad leg and he thought, "Please! Please let me find that the snapping noise was a branch breaking." Slowly he moved his hand to the area of the break and when he touched it, more pain shot out and he could feel the familiar bump; he had re-broken the leg. "No! No!" he screamed. "This can't be happening. I was being so careful, so cautious."

Carefully, he slid back and worked his legs out of the crevice. The cast was still firmly in place, but it was now painfully apparent that he should have used heavier wood. The soft pine sticks had bowed from the pressure when he fell. As he started loosening the ropes on the cast, the pain eased, but the lump caused by the break stayed.

Sitting in the snow, he cursed his bad luck. Why didn't he stay on the ground and pull himself backwards through the brush. It wouldn't have taken much longer than the hobbling he was doing. After all, he had gotten along just fine for the last few weeks by staying on the ground. Soon he realized that it was pointless to think of what might have been. He had another decision to make.

The cabin was still in view. He could crawl back, re-set the leg and build a better cast. But the ordeal he went through on the first break was still fresh in his mind. He knew it could delay him several days and he wouldn't make it to the lake on time. And the thought of returning to the cabin terrified him. It was like being in prison. No...worse than prison. In prison, you get three square meals a day and proper medical care. Broken leg or not, he was a free man and refused to go back to that torture chamber.

Sitting on the ground, he spun around and pointed his back north. Then, using his hands like canoe paddles, started bulldozing through the brush and snow with his legs dragging behind. After going only twenty feet, his

160

broken leg felt like it was on fire. Unable to bear the pain any longer, he stopped and loosened the splint ropes.

Chapter 18

Back To Prison

It was becoming obvious that he could never reach the lake. He'd die in the woods and the wolves would gobble up his remains. As much as he dreaded going back to the cabin, it was a life or death choice and the cabin meant life. He wouldn't be at the lake on New Years, but surely Jack was a good enough woodsman that he'd find and rescue him. Turning around, he started pushing his way back to camp.

When he reached the ledge above the camp, he slid down backwards and with a final effort, pulled himself inside the cabin. He remembered that he had left the pack and rifle behind, but he could always retrieve it later. Right now, he needed a pain killer. Reaching into the rafters, he pulled down the bottle of moonshine. It was getting empty, but fortunately, Jack had sent two along.

After scrambling his brain into a drunken stupor, he dug out the leg lever he used before. As he held it in his hands, it looked like an evil instrument of torture. He hated the thing and vowed to break it into a million pieces when the ordeal was over. Repeating the process of three weeks earlier, he snapped the leg back in place, tightened the ropes, then screamed and hollered and cursed and drank until the pain subsided and he was able to sleep.

When he awoke the next day, he felt awful. Fever wracked his body so bad that he wanted to die. He stayed in bed for days, getting up only to light an occasional fire or grab a piece of venison. The days passed quickly as he drifted in and out of consciousness. Finally, on the 5th day, the fever broke and he was able to stay awake.

As he X'd out the missing dates on the calendar, he found it was New Years Day or somewhere close. Jack was probably at the lake right now, looking for him and wondering what happened. Of course, he would then hike in, find the trapline and follow it to the cabin. "He'll be a bit upset when he gets here," he thought. "I'll get a long lecture about how I can't handle myself in the woods. But I've saved him some venison and moonshine and he'll soon be in a good spirits."

Several days passed and Jack still hadn't arrived. As Mittens peeked out the cabin door, he noticed big flakes of snow falling. The snow continued all day and by midnight, the temperature dropped and a howling wind started whipping the white stuff around. By morning, it was a full blown blizzard and he wondered if Jack would be able to find him. "He'll have to wait out the blizzard before he can look for me," he thought. "I hope he found shelter."

After a few days, the wind went down and the sun came out. He tried opening the door, but the snow was packed so tight against it that it wouldn't budge. "That was kind of dumb of me," he thought. "If I ever build another cabin, I'll make the door swing in instead of out." After beating on the door awhile, he was able to get his arm through and pushed enough snow away to poke his head out. As he looked outside, he was stunned; the blizzard had obliterated everything. The neatly shoveled camp was buried under several feet of snow and you couldn't see the trails.

After marveling at all the snow, his thoughts switched to Jack. "How will he find me in all this snow? The trapping trails will be drifted shut. There'll be nothing out there to direct him to the cabin and he'd have to be standing on the roof to spot it. Plus, he only has a vague notion of where I'm trapping. For all he knows, I could be a mile from here."

The more he thought of it, the more he realized how dire his predicament was. "Jack could wander the woods all winter and never find me," he thought. And why should he even try? After all, he thinks I'm a greenhorn who doesn't know the woods. When he got to the lake and I wasn't there, he probably figured I did myself in. He probably left and figured he'd come back in the spring and pick up his traps."

He started weighing his options. He was almost out of food and firewood; The cabin was buried under tons of snow, but that was good. Like a snow cave, it would be insulated from extreme temperatures and he could survive without firewood. But he had to find food. Perhaps when his leg felt better, he could get outside and set some rabbit snares. If he could hold out another month he could try to reach the lake. Then another thought hit him: What good would it do to get to the lake? No one would be there and then he'd be in a worse fix than he was already in. The situation was desperate. His only hope was that somehow, some way, Jack would find him. If not, he would slowly starve to death.

A few more days passed and another storm came. This time, the wind howled for almost two days straight. Unable to reach his woodpile, he stayed bundled up in bed, waiting out the storm. Finally the blizzard passed, and again, he tried to open the door. This time it was stuck tighter than the jaws of a bear trap. After beating on it for several minutes he managed to open it a crack. But the snow was piled so high above the door, he couldn't tell if it was night or day outside.

Grabbing the railroad cop night stick, he poked it through the crack of the doorway. After probing around a bit, he yanked it out and a shaft of light beamed through. "Well, I've got my work cut out for me today," he thought. "It will probably take all day to get this door open." Taking the shotgun down from the rafters, he unloaded it and shoved the butt end through the opening. It made a neat snow pusher and after an hour he had a fairly large hole punched through. Finally he was able to squeeze his hand through the doorway and grab at the snow behind the door.

As he continued picking away, he thought he heard a faint buzzing sound — like a mosquito. "Must be my brains rattling around," he mused as he continued clawing bits of snow from behind the door. But the noise kept coming back, then fading away. Soon the sound became unmistakable: "Ohmigosh!" he yelled. "It's an airplane. Jack sent a plane to rescue me."

The excitement of hearing the plane was quickly tempered by another thought: "They won't be able to see my camp under all this snow. I've got to get outside and signal them." Frantically, he pushed and shoved the door, but it still wouldn't budge. As the sound got louder, he became more frantic. Feeling like a person buried alive in a coffin, he clawed desperately at the snow in the doorway.

Finally he leaned back and kicked the door repeatedly with his good leg until it opened a couple more inches. Shoving his arm through the opening, he reached behind the door, grabbed handfuls of snow and pulled them inside the cabin until the door opened further. As he stuck his head through the opening, he

167

could see the plane — a bright red Curtiss Robin on skis — circling around, apparently looking for him.

The sound of the plane faded slightly as it headed east and circled Arrow Lake. Suddenly it became louder as it turned towards the cabin. As the noise increased, he clawed at the snow faster, then pushing up as hard as he could, tried to shove his body through the opening. But with only one good leg, he couldn't do it.

The noise increased to a loud racket as the plane headed straight for the camp. Flying close to treetop level, it suddenly burst into view — directly over the cabin. The barking sound of the 200 horsepower radial engine blasted his eardrums and the prop wash blew snow off the treetops as it sped across the camp. As a white flurry of snow fluttered down on him, he yelled, "Come back! I'm here. I'm alive." But he was wasting his breath.

Wiggling his head and shoulders back inside the cabin, he thought, "This can't be true. It can't be happening to me. I've opened that door a thousand times and now when I desperately need it open, it won't move. If I can't signal them, they'll think I'm dead and leave me here to rot." Frantically searching for a way out, he grabbed his axe and viciously chopped at the door. But the door bounced each time he struck it — limiting the penetration of the axe. Worse yet, with each reverberating blow, more snow tumbled against the door forcing it closed again.

Pausing to catch his breath, he could see that things

were getting worse, so he went back to clawing the snow with his hand. After a few minutes he removed the snow that tumbled down from the axe pounding, but he still could only get one arm and his head through the opening. In the distance he could still see the plane, but now it sounded like a mosquito again.

Suddenly the noise grew louder — the plane was coming back. As it came closer, Mittens stared at it in frustration. Finally the solution hit him: "That's it! I've got to start a fire in the stove. Then they'll see the smoke. Why didn't I think of that sooner?" Pulling himself back inside the cabin, he frantically looked for something, anything to burn. There was no wood and even if there was, there wouldn't be enough time to light it. "The moonshine! That's it," he thought. "It's almost pure alcohol and should burn."

Quickly grabbing the bottle, he poured some of the liquid in the stove and struck a match. It burned, but it was almost smokeless; they'd never see it. Grabbing his knife, he dived for the bed, cut a large chunk of cloth from the bedding and soaked it with moonshine. While he stuffed it into the stove, the sound of the plane intensified. As he struck a match, the material started to burn while the plane made a low pass over the swamp — directly in front of the cabin. After the plane passed, black smoke rolled out of the chimney, but it was too late.

Sticking his head out the door, he watched the plane in the distance as it made steep turns and circles near

Lake Isabella. "OK fellows," he thought. "The next time you come over, this smoke is going to smack you right in the windshield." The sound of the plane grew fainter as it followed the Isabella River. As he shoved more chunks of bedding into the stove, the smoke pipe belched black smoke like the stack on a brick factory. When he looked out again, he couldn't see the plane but he could still hear a faint buzzing in the distance. Then the noise faded further until a deathly silence returned.

At first he refused to believe the plane would leave without finding him and he kept the fire smoldering while he continued clearing snow from the door. After an hour he was able to reach behind the door with a shovel and move the snow completely away. Using the door for support, he stood up and viewed the surroundings. The snow was piled in huge drifts that covered every trace of the camp. "No wonder they couldn't see me," he thought.

Assuming the plane would be back, he started carving a big SOS in the snow. Unwilling to risk slipping and falling on his injured leg, he sat on the camp stool while shoveling out the first "S". When the letter collapsed, he decided to shovel a large rectangle, then use ashes from the stove to spell SOS. By nightfall, the opening was half cleared and it became apparent that the plane had returned to base for refueling and wouldn't be back that day. He decided to finish the SOS in the morning.

Convinced that rescue was close at hand, he ate a double ration of venison that night. It was the first time in weeks that he had a full stomach and he thought, "Tomorrow I'll be in town eating blueberry pie." In his heart he didn't believe this, but his mind, trying to prepare him for a terrible letdown, clung to the belief that the plane would return.

By noon the next day, he completed the shoveling and spelled out the SOS. The bottle of moonshine, rags and matches were close by as he sat in the doorway and patiently listened for the sound of the plane. But the only sound to break the silence was the call of a raven and the constant ringing in his ears.

Chapter 19

Will Tomorrow Come

That night, reality began to sink in: the plane would not be back. He had blown what may have been his only chance of rescue. Stranded in the wilderness with a bad leg and shrinking food supply, his wilderness dream was being shattered and the cabin he worked so hard to build was slowly becoming his tomb.

Glancing at his calendar, he took stock of the situation. It was the middle of January, food in the cabin was nearly gone and there was a five day supply in his pack which was still in the woods —100 yards from camp. He figured he could stretch the pack to ten days and squeeze a few more meals from the pile of venison bones and tallow he had saved for the dog. Plus, he could set a few snares around camp and catch rabbits.

173

There might be enough food to make it through another month, but with three more months of winter, that wouldn't be enough. He continued to hold out hope that Jack would come to his rescue.

With his leg still bothering him, he decided to hold off retrieving the pack and try getting by with the food on hand. Crawling out to the food locker, he took inventory. There were a couple packages of venison he didn't know he had and several slabs of tallow plus the hide and bones. To get more mileage from the food, he put a bone in the cook pot followed by a chunk of tallow, then a small chunk of venison cut into tiny bits. He was out of firewood, so he shaved strips of pine from the log walls inside the cabin for fuel.

After bringing this gourmet delight to a boil, he tasted it. It was awful. Fortunately, Jack sent along lots of salt and after giving it a generous dose, he was able to down the tallow and chew the remaining meat from the bone. The soup that remained would be his next meal. After a few days, he couldn't stand eating any more of this witches potion and decided to set rabbit snares and try to retrieve the pack.

As he crawled through the doorway, his bad leg bumped the door and a shot of pain hit him. Three weeks had passed since re-breaking the leg and it was still sensitive, swollen and sore. The starvation diet was taking a toll on the healing process and he had to treat the leg like it was freshly broken. Not wanting to risk breaking it a third time, he decided to stay on the ground

174

and slide all the way to the pack. Using the deer hide as a sled, he sat on the hide and pushed himself backwards with his hands.

After inching up the rock ledge, the going got easier and after an hour of bulldozing backwards through the deep snow, he reached the area where he left the pack. It was buried in the snow but he could see the rifle barrel sticking out. Suddenly, a chill raced through his body and he froze in terror: a wolf was watching him.

Standing in the brush just 50 feet away was Devil Eyes, the black wolf. He was crouched low and his golden eyes were glaring at Mittens. "Why is he stalking me," he thought. "It was Millie he was after, not me. Is he waiting for me to die so he can eat me?" After a moment, he yelled, "I'm not dead yet!" Then he lunged for the rifle, pulled it from the pack and levered a cartridge into the chamber. By the time he drew a bead on the wolf, it was gone. "That beast is smart — almost human," he thought.

After retrieving the pack, he turned around and started back. He had turned up several sticks of wood while pushing through the snow and stuck them in the pack for firewood. After dragging the pack back to the cabin, he ventured out again, setting eight rabbit snares in a circle around camp. That night, he cooked a small piece of venison steak. With the taste of the terrible broth from the last few days still lingering in his throat, the venison was a real treat.

The next morning while checking his snares, he

175

was shocked to find that three were tripped but the rabbits were gone. The wolves had stolen them from the snares, ate them and left behind the legs and heads. "You stinkin creatures chased all the deer from the area, killed my dog and caused my broken leg," he yelled. "And you're still not happy. You want everything including the little bit of food I need to survive."

Picking up the rabbit leftovers and a few more scraps of wood, he sledded back to the cabin. After carving away some of the unpleasant features of the rabbit heads and feet, he tossed them into the pot, added water and brought it to a boil. It didn't taste too bad and required less salt than the tallow soup. But there was so little of it that it hardly whetted his appetite. "This is ridiculous," he thought. "Eating leftovers that the wolves don't want. I wonder what a wolf tastes like? Probably better than rabbit heads." The thought intrigued him. He had never seen wolf steak listed on a restaurant menu, but to a starving person, it could be the Chefs "special of the day."

He knew he was wasting time trying to trap them — they were too smart. And, if he carried a gun, they knew enough to stay away. "What if I figure out a way to hide the gun," he thought. "Then when one shows up, I'll whip it out and nail him." Grabbing a pair of old pants, he ripped off one of the legs and made a case to hide the gun. Placing the gun between his legs, it blended in and looked like part of his pants. After a bit of practice, he was able to do a fast draw and bring the rifle to shooting position in seconds. "Tomorrow the menu is wolf," he declared.

In mid-morning, he slid out of the cabin, sat on his deerskin sled and pushed his way into the woods using a new contraption he invented: a small pair of hand snowshoes that he made from pine and deerskin. The snow had settled a bit and with the wide hand devices, he increased his speed to turtle velocity and extended his travel range further from the cabin.

He had cleaned out most of the rabbits near the cabin, but with his new found mobility, he was able to move some of the snares deeper into the woods. This gave him access to more firewood, but towing it back to the cabin zapped his strength. The daily two hour trips into the woods were leaving him totally exhausted as the lack of food continued to take a toll. Although he kept a constant watch for wolves, all he saw were their tracks and they continued stealing his rabbits.

After a few days he was out of food. With the pungent cooking odors fading from the cabin, another smell was replacing it: body odor. "Wow! This place smells worse than Jack's house," he joked. "If I don't clean up, they probably won't let me on the plane when they rescue me." Tossing wood in the stove, he built a fire and soon the cabin was warm enough to remove his clothing. After boiling a kettle of water and peeling off his shirt, he was stunned when he looked at his bare chest. He had lost so much weight that he could count his rib bones.

177

He had been losing weight all fall and called it a healthy loss each time he re-notched his belt buckle. But there was nothing healthy about this — he was downright skinny. His 300 pound frame had shrunk to just a shell of what he once was and bones were sticking out everywhere. As he removed his pants, he received a bigger shock: his newly formed "legs of steel" had turned into toothpicks. After weeks without use, the muscles on his broken leg had shrunk to nearly nothing and the skin had shriveled up like a prune. The swelling around the break and the bulging of the knee made the leg resemble a snake that swallowed a couple mice.

"I've gotta eat," he mumbled. "I have to find something, anything." Suddenly, he had an idea: the beaver pelts. When he scraped and stretched them, he didn't do a good job and a lot of fat remained on the hides. Crawling out to the hide rack, he cut the anchor rope and a pile of frozen hides tumbled down. Dragging a bundle inside, he thawed them out and started scraping. Soon, he had a cupful of fat which he dumped in the cookpot. To give it body, he removed the claws and hair from the feet and tossed them in.

As the mixture came to a boil, it gave off a foul odor. With the stench nearly overwhelming him, he poured some of the rancid mixture into a cup, smothered it with salt and took a swallow. It immediately came up. Even in his emaciated condition, he couldn't hold this terrible stuff down. Realizing he had to drink it or die, he added one more ingredient: moonshine. When he poured it into the pot, the powerful liquid churned, boiled and bubbled while it battled the beaver brew for dominance of the cooking pot. The moonshine won and when the mixture cooled, he was able to consume and hold it down.

He awoke the next morning feeling sick. His stomach was still churning from the terrible evening meal and his head felt like it was being squeezed in a vise. The beaver brew helped, but he needed real food. Grabbing his rifle, he crawled onto the deer skin sled and headed out to check his snares. He hadn't seen fresh wolf tracks for a few days and with the competition out of the area, his hopes were high for catching rabbits. But after checking the snares, he found he only caught one. Pushing back to the cabin, his arms became tired and he had to stop and rest often. Rather than wait for supper, he cooked the rabbit immediately. It didn't fill his stomach, but anything was better than beaver fat.

He had planned to go to Arrow Lake to fish when his leg healed, but with the leg still sore and swollen and the snow hip deep, he knew it would be hopeless to try. And, with his arm strength failing, it wasn't even an option; he barely had the strength to check his rabbit traps. The only choice was to stay at the cabin and try to live off the hides and rabbits.

A few more days passed and the situation got worse: he couldn't get up the rock ledge and into the woods to check the snares and it took all of his strength to retrieve and scrape more hides. When he ran out of

179

wood, he went back to chiseling strips of pine from the logs inside the cabin. As the rounded logs slowly became flat sided, he started hollowing them. Each day became a challenge to stay alive as the pain in his stomach became worse and the constant ringing in his ears got louder.

Checking the calendar, he saw that February had arrived. Somehow he survived a whole month with barely any food. But he was at the end of his rope. He couldn't stand the torture another week, much less several more months. Too frail to leave the cabin, he stayed in bed day and night, rising occasionally to carve out firewood and try to eat beaver fat. He often fantasized that he was a bear and wished that he could curl up in a state of hibernation, sleep through the winter and awaken to the sounds of spring.

Chapter 20

The Will To Live

The first days of February turned into agony. The bed was his only sanctuary from the relentless cold and even that was failing. With his body reduced to skin and bones, the blankets and furs no longer kept him warm. As he trembled from the cold, while huddling in bed, loneliness and solitude haunted him. Every grueling minute seemed like an hour and a day seemed like a year. The terrible quiet and the never ending ringing in his ears were breaking his spirit and he no longer cared if he lived or died.

By the first week of February, he accepted the fact that rescue wasn't coming and in a few days, his suffering would end. Unable to bear the thought of another day of torture, he decided to speed up the process. Straining his shriveled body, he reached into the rafters and pulled out the rifle. Cradling it in his hands, he thought of how the gun had helped him when he badly needed a deer and how it brought him comfort when he feared the wolves. Then he thought of how it was now failing to bring him the food he so desperately needed. Ironically, the gun would now be used to free him from the bonds of this icy prison and release his tortured soul to places unknown.

With his face to the barrel, panic gripped him. Everything he learned in life flashed through his brain, screaming, shouting and pleading, "Don't do it!" His hand stiffened and he couldn't pull the trigger. "A note," he thought. "I have to leave a note and tell Jack, or whoever finds me, what happened." With pen and paper, he started scrawling out a message:

Feb. 7, 1932

To my good friend Jack,

I tried to meet you on New Years but broke my leg and couldn't get to the lake. I have used up the last of my food and cannot continue any longer. You can keep my share of the furs and anything else that's mine.

I saw your plane come over last month. You couldn't see me because the blizzard had covered...

Suddenly a thought entered his mind: "Jack is an experienced woodsman. He should have known how tough it would be to locate a camp after a blizzard. Why didn't he wait a day or two, give me a chance to make the camp visible, then come back with the plane and try again? Could it be that he was too thrifty? After all, he'd have to pay a pilot 25 bucks for each trip. What other reason could there be for not trying again?"

His body was ravished by hunger and his life hung by a thread, but his mind was as clear as the waters of the Ahmoo. "Could it be that a mans worth is measured not in dollars, but by the efforts spent on his rescue?" he thought. "If that's true, then is my value on earth equal to the price of one plane trip?"

He didn't want to believe it, but the answer was obvious: Jack had purchased one plane trip in a half-hearted effort to find him — and to convince others that he tried. "When Spring arrives, he'll come back, pick up his traps and bury my bones," thought Mittens. "Then, he'll take my share of the furs and have a wild time at my expense. And if anyone asks about me, he'll just say I was a dumb kid who couldn't handle himself in the woods."

After ripping up the note, his first thought was to burn the furs to prevent Jack from profiting from his demise. But getting the furs to burn would be tough. The only solution was to stay alive. Somehow, some way, he had to stay alive and make it through the winter. With newly found determination, he put the rifle back in the rafters, grabbed the pot of beaver fat and started forcing it into his mouth.

After shivering in bed all night, he awoke to find that he had survived another day. And it would be a nice day with no wind and the sun warmly shining. Cracking open the cabin door, he felt the warmth of the sun on his face and it felt good. He decided to try to check his rabbit snares. Climbing onto his deerskin sled, he pushed with his weak bony arms and slowly slid towards the rock ledge. When he reached the ledge, he collapsed and leaned against it for hours, absorbing the warm rays of the sun and trying to sleep.

As the sun sank lower, the temperature fell and he crawled back into the cabin to face another night of terror. A night that would seem like an eternity. He hardly had the strength to lift the kettle as he forced down the last of the beaver broth. If the stuff was keeping him alive, he couldn't tell. The only fuel powering his body was his obsession to even the score with Jack. An obsession that was weakening by the hour.

Two days had passed since his suicide attempt and his condition had reached a new low. It was a cold and overcast day: not one for sitting outside. But it didn't matter. Unable to get out of bed, he laid in a pitiful state of semi-consciousness —shivering from the cold and wishing for an end to the awful misery. By the middle of the day, thoughts of revenge departed his brain — taking with it his will to live.

Sliding his tortured body out of bed, he reached up and pulled the rifle down from the rafters. "Jack, you win," he mumbled. "I wouldn't wish this on anyone else, but I wish you could see what you put me through. Someday your time will come and when it does, I hope..." Suddenly his thoughts were interrupted by a noise. There was no wind, but he thought he heard a branch break outside.

Placing the rifle on the floor, he slid to the door and cracked it open. "Snap..Bam!" came sounds from the brush. "What in the world is making the noise?" he thought, as he stretched further through the door to get a better look. "Ohmigosh!" he mumbled, as he stared in disbelief. "A moose!" Rubbing his cloudy eyes, he looked again. It was a large bull moose walking slowly out of the brush and into the swamp next to the cabin. Grabbing the rifle, he poked the barrel through the doorway. The moose continued walking, then stopped — 100 feet from the cabin.

With trembling hands, he lined up the sights. "Please! Please don't let me miss," he pleaded. Suddenly another thought went through his mind: if he simply shot the moose, it would likely run hundreds of yards into the woods and die. In his weakened condition, he'd be unable to go after it. He had to make a difficult head shot and drop the animal in its tracks.

The moose burrowed its head into the snow, looking for grass, then raised it back up and sniffed the air. With the rifle pressed firmly against the cabin wall for steadiness, he fired. The moose stiffened and shook its huge head — as if unhurt. Mittens levered another round in and fired again, and again and again. Suddenly the huge bull took two steps forward and collapsed. "I did it! I did it!" he cried, as he leaned back and started

to sob.

His heart was pounding like a hammer as he slid his shriveled body out of the cabin. Then, straining his weakened muscles to the limit, crawled through the deep snow to the large brown mound of fur that was to be his salvation. Acting like a starving wolf, he ripped into the side of the moose with his knife, tore out a chunk of meat and crammed it into his mouth. In beastly fashion he ripped at it again, then continued eating until his shriveled up stomach rejected the intrusion and shoved it all out.

Huddled against the warm mass of the carcass, he stopped to think: "All this food and I can't eat it?" Deciding on a slower approach, he stuck a few large chunks of meat in his pocket and after partially field dressing the carcass, started back to the cabin. On the way, he hit another jackpot: his path uncovered a downed jackpine he had previously overlooked — enough firewood for several meals. Lady Luck had dealt him a fresh hand.

Cutting the meat into tiny pieces, he fried them to a dark crisp color and gulped one down, quickly following it with water. The delicious smell of the freshly fried moose was overwhelming, but he managed to wait 10 minutes between bites to condition his stomach. After an hour of slow and cautious nibbling while basking in the heat of a warm cabin, he started getting drowsy. Crawling into bed, he slept for the first time in several days.

187

After a couple hours of sleep, he was up again, frying more steak. His muscles were weak and his bum leg ached, but his spirits were soaring as he increased his food intake. Soon he had eaten both pieces of moose and could feel his stomach growing. Struggling out of the cabin, he crawled back to the moose carcass to complete the field dressing. This time he brought back four big slices and more firewood.

That night he was able to eat a large slab of moose without a stomach rebellion. "I'm gonna make it," he said. "I'm gonna make it out of here and settle the score with Jack." But his growing confidence was tempered by the thought of how terribly close he came to ending it all. If the moose hadn't shown up when it did, would he be alive now? If his newly found hatred of Jack hadn't kept him going a few extra days, would he still be living? His answer was simple: "It wasn't my time."

Chapter 21

Revenge Part 2

Two days had passed since he shot the moose and he could feel his weight and strength returning. Scooting out to the moose and back was becoming easy, and with an animal that big, there was no need to ration — there was more than enough meat to last until the ice out in April. By then his leg would be healed and he could pack up and leave.

While sitting contentedly in the cabin, enjoying his good fortune, he heard a noise outside. Peeking through the door opening, he could see movement near the moose: the wolves were back and they wanted his moose. It was too dark to clearly see them so he fired the rifle in the air to scare them off. A half hour later they were back, so he yelled and shot again. They left and returned again.

He wasn't in a mood for sharing, especially with those two, so he sat up most of the night guarding his prize. The wolves, ravaged by hunger, were becoming accustomed to the gunfire and returning frequently. Desperate to get some sleep, he dragged firewood out to the moose, built a fire and slept next to the carcass. When daylight came, he checked the moose and was appalled by the amount of meat the wolves had taken. They were doing far more than nibbling: they were ripping off big chunks, dragging it away for storage and coming back for more.

He knew that trying to trap them would be a waste of time, so he stayed in the cabin, hoping to get a clear shot at them. The moose was lying close to a dense grove of spruce where the wolves hid. When they came out to steal meat, both kept an eye on the cabin door and the instant it moved, they'd duck back into the spruce trees. It was turning into a game of cat and mouse and the wolves were winning.

Something had to be done — quickly. At the rate the wolves were stealing meat, the entire carcass could be gone in a few days and he'd be starving again. His only choice was to try to move the meat to the cabin. Working all day, he hacked away at the carcass until his pack was full, then wrestled the heavy pack back to the cabin and returned for more. When darkness came, he built a series of fires and kept working. Whenever he got sleepy, he stopped and stared into the nearby spruce trees and when the firelight revealed sets of eyes watching him, he would suddenly become wide awake.

After working all night and half of the next day, the locker was full and extra meat was stacked outside the door. Satisfied he had enough to last until spring, he went to bed and slept for hours. When he awoke, the wolves were ripping away at the moose again and by the time he got the gun, they were gone. Gritting his teeth in frustration, he came up with a new plan: "Why stay in the cabin?" he thought. "Since they're watching me here, why don't I build a blind away from the cabin and hide there?"

He decided to give it a try. Selecting a dense patch of brush 50 feet from the moose, he started cutting and weaving spruce boughs. Soon, he had a dense wall of spruce to hide behind, a log to sit on and a small opening to stick his rifle through.

When the wolves came back to feed, they spotted the new blind right away and cautiously circled and checked it out. Mittens knew they'd do that, so he stayed away. Soon, the wolves got used to the new blind and gave it only an occasional glance. The next day, after chasing the wolves away, he noticed that the wind was blowing toward the blind and would cover his scent. "Now's the time," he said.

Sneaking into the blind, he bundled up with a blanket and sat on the log with his rifle ready. After waiting a little over an hour, the wolf he called "Gray Ghost" appeared, followed by "Devil Eyes". With the

191

wind favoring him, they couldn't catch his scent and started feeding on the moose. "This is too good to be true," he thought, as he poked the gun barrel through the opening and took aim at Devil Eyes.

"This one's for Millie," he mumbled, as he pulled back the hammer of the gun. Hearing the metallic clink of the hammer cocking, Devil Eyes spun around and looked at the pile of spruce where the noise came from. But as the wolf stared at the spruce, he didn't know he was looking down the barrel of a gun. And he couldn't see the twinkle in Mittens' eye, or hear the muffled sound that said, "At last! I've got you."

As he started to pull the trigger, his hand froze and he couldn't shoot. Just like his suicide attempt, something inside of him was shouting, "No! Don't do it." He tried again, but couldn't fire. Grabbing a branch, he pulled himself up and stood in plain view of the wolf. Devil Eyes lowered his head and glared at him with a look on his face that seemed to say, "Leave me alone and I'll leave you alone." As the wolf turned and trotted away, Mittens yelled, "Bang! I got you."

When the elation eased from his "catch and release" victory, he stood and stared at the spot where the wolf stood. He was baffled. "Why couldn't I shoot?" he thought. "What made me stop?" Mittens had always divided life on the planet into three separate categories: The first was human life, which was sacred. The second, pet life, was also sacred. Everything else — from wood tick to whale — were lumped into a third group he called "food" and he often argued with Mrs. Larsen when she tried to create more categories. Now, he wasn't sure.

"Could it be that this crafty creature snuck out of my 'food' category and slipped inside the sacred status I've set aside for humans and pets?" he wondered. "Or, is it because I have all the food I need and he's no longer a threat? After all, I'm an outsider entering his home and all he wants to do is survive — just like me." With multiple doubts and questions calling for rational thoughts and answers, he shrugged his shoulders and headed back to the cabin.

With no one shooting at them, the wolves became braver and returned to the moose carcass often. Soon, they were ignoring Mittens completely and he often sat outside and watched them feed. When the carcass got lighter, he dragged it closer to the cabin so he could observe them better. Longing for companionship and not very fussy about the company he kept, he decided to try to make friends with the wolves. As he continued moving the carcass closer to the cabin, he thought, "Pretty soon I'll have them eating out of my hand." Following an afternoon feeding, he dragged the carcass to a spot just twenty feet from the cabin. Unwilling to enlist in his "Lonely Hearts Club", the wolves dragged the carcass away and he never saw them again.

Chapter 22

A New Day Dawning

With a steady serving of three meals a day, he was recovering his strength and body weight quickly and the swelling in his broken leg was going away. He could have resumed walking earlier, but took no chances and continued moving around camp on his deerskin sled. As the days dragged on, he kept busy building different types of sleds — trying to find the perfect combination that would propel him around the woods faster.

As the weeks wore on, the temperature started to rise. "I'm going to make it," he yelled, as he awoke one morning to the sound of water dripping from the roof. Winter was losing its grip and he could feel spring coming. Using a cane, he started walking upright around camp, but still used the sled in deep snow and rarely removed the protective pine braces from his leg. The hard crust that formed on the snow made it easy to slide around and a couple times he considered traveling to the lake to go fishing, but common sense prevailed.

April came and the snow melt increased. Water was running off the rocky ledge so fast it was flooding the floor of the cabin, forcing him to move to a lean-to shelter on higher ground. As the swamp turned into a small lake, he cached his food supply in a tree and emptied the cabin. Brown patches of grass were appearing almost everywhere as the snow continued melting. With his broken leg healed and ready for a field test, he decided to go on a hike.

The next morning, after tightly splinting his leg with thick pieces of pine, he grabbed his cane, hobbled out of camp and headed into the woods. After picking his way around the remaining snowbanks and over the rocky terrain, he arrived at the Ahmoo Creek — next to his favorite boulder. The boulder that brought him joy and comfort when he was sad. The boulder that gave him courage and inspiration when he had problems. And...the boulder that dragged him down and drowned his dream in the ice cold waters of the Ahmoo.

Standing by the base of the boulder, he placed his hand on its lichen crusted surface and looked up. A chill went through his body and he vowed never to climb it again. Walking to the other side of the boulder, he found a flat rock facing the creek and sat down to watch the water flow.

It seemed like years had passed since he last saw this place. Except for the boiling water that now raced through the creek, nothing had changed. The teetering rocks were still balanced on the edge of the twin falls — resisting the powerful flow of the spring runoff. As he gazed at the rocks, he wondered: "If I ever return, will the teetering rocks still be there? Or will a passing visitor roll them into the creek — just to hear the splash?"

Walking up to the pile of rocks that covered Millie, he paused and said, "Well old girl, I sure miss you. I could have killed those nasty wolves for you, but I let 'em go. Hope you don't mind." Seeing a bright colored object in the grass, he walked over and picked it up. It was Millie's ball. Walking back to the grave, he placed the ball on the pile of stones, took another look at his favorite boulder, then walked away and never returned.

* * * * *

Another week went by and the snow was reduced to scattered patches. With the ice on the lakes ready to break up, he decided to get ready for packing out. Still worried about his leg, he blazed a different trail to Lake Insula that was longer, but safer to hike. After a few days of hacking away brush, he arrived at the lake and found it was still locked in ice.

Looking around, he spotted the canoes, flipped them over and located the message bottle. The bottle was empty which meant that Jack had been there, read his note but didn't leave a reply. "At least I know he was here on New Years," he thought. "And more than likely it was him in the plane. But it still doesn't tell me why he didn't try a second time. All I know for sure is when I get back to Winton and walk into his house, only one of us is going to walk out."

After working his temper to a boil, he grabbed his gear and stormed off down his new trail. Although it was longer, the trail was a breeze to hike and as nightfall neared, he picked up the pace so he'd reach camp before dark. Suddenly he tripped on a rock and went flying forward. As he crashed to the ground, the weight of his body slammed against his injured leg and he heard a loud "Crack!"

"No! No! Not again," he cried, as he slowly placed his hand on the injured area. It was smooth and without a bump. Carefully, he stood up, kicked the leg a bit, then looked at the ground. Laughing out loud, he reached down and picked up the stick that he had just fallen on. As he gave the broken stick a toss, he said, "Sorry Jack, but you'll have to do better than that."

The next day he went out on the trapline to retrieve traps. With the creeks boiling over from the spring thaw, each crossing became an adventure, often requiring lengthy hikes to locate places to cross. His body was still frail from the winter ordeal and he could carry only a half filled pack. But each daily hike made him a little stronger and every night he gorged himself with enough moose meat to feed a pack of wolves. After a week he had all the traps collected and started to feel like his old self again.

With the traps collected, he started breaking camp. During the long winter months, he had whittled out a wooden towing sled — complete with rollers to ease it over the rough ground. After loading the sled with gear, he commenced the two mile drag to the lake, dumped the gear and returned for more. After a few days of hauling, he loaded the last bundle and prepared to leave.

Standing on the ledge overlooking the cabin, he took one last look at the camp. Suddenly it occurred to him, "Hey! I already did this. A few days before New Years, I stood on this same spot and said good-bye to this place. And look what happened! This time I'm really leaving," he chuckled as he grabbed the sled rope and started dragging.

The ice was gone from Echo Bay as he packed the two canoes for the long trip to Winton. Every inch of space was taken up and again, the canoes floated deep in the water. "Good thing I lost weight and ate all the fat from those hides," he joked. "Otherwise I'd need a third canoe." As he pushed away from shore, he paused, cupped his hands around his mouth and yelled, "Good-bye Mittens!" As the forest echoed a fond farewell, he dipped his paddle in the water and headed west.

The sun glowed warmly and the wind was calm as the canoes glided across the glass smooth surface of the lake. For a while he thought this day would never come, but at last it had arrived. He was heading home. The small problem that he had no home to go to didn't

199

bother him. Entranced by the beauty of the lake and happy to be alive, he wasn't sure if he was heading for home or leaving his home.

The next day, while struggling to move the heavy load to the other end of a portage, he thought about the furs and how much they were worth. With money jingling in his pockets from his half share, he could leave Winton in style — riding a passenger train instead of a boxcar. On a couple occasions he had thought of selling the furs, pocketing all the money and make Jack go back to Insula and haul the traps and gear back himself. But in spite of everything, he decided to stick to the deal. He'd haul it all out and split the fur money fairly. But he had a little surprise planned for that low life bandit.

With the portage nearly completed, he grabbed the last canoe and headed down the path. Halfway there, he spotted movement up ahead. Thinking it was a bear, he dropped the canoe and prepared to defend himself. But it wasn't a bear. It was a group of people. The first humans he had seen in nearly a year were walking toward him. The leader was a guide who was taking a group on an early spring fishing trip.

Having gone so long without talking to anyone but himself, his dog and an occasional wolf, he was apprehensive. He also hadn't looked in a mirror for a long time. Whiskers and windburn hid his babyface cheeks, causing him to look far older than he was. Pine sticks tied to his leg and a leather towing harness decorated his ragged, filthy clothes. With a rifle slung over his shoulder and a policeman's nightstick dangling from his belt, this normally timid person looked very intimidating.

"Hello stranger!" greeted the guide. "That's quite a load you're packing out. I mean no offense, but you look like you've been out there for quite a while."

"Yah," replied Mittens. "Longer than I cared to."

"Where are you heading for?"

"Winton...to see a guy named Jack Denley."

"Wow! You really have been gone a long time. Haven't you heard? Jack died in a plane crash several months ago."

Devastated by the news, Mittens replied, "Wha...Wha...What happened?"

"It was back in January. Jack hired Buzz Mattson to fly him around. They say he was looking for a lost trapper near Lake Isabella. But knowing Jack, he was probably trying to poach a moose or something from the plane. They didn't find anything, then tried again a few days later. No one is sure what happened, but on that second trip the plane went down near Gabbro Lake. Buzz had a bad habit of flying low and probably clipped a tree. They figured that neither guy was hurt that bad, but it took almost a month to find the plane. When they did, both were dead from cold and starvation."

"That's awful," said Mittens. "I can't believe he's

201

gone."

"Yah, that was a tough one to take; Buzz had a lot of friends. And, he was one of the best pilots around — won a silver cross in the war. A lot of folks felt bad about losing him.

No one shed any tears for old Jack, though. That bum was about as worthless as they come. In fact, I'll bet that's why you're looking for him — to collect money. Am I right?"

Standing in stunned silence, Mittens stared coldly at the guide.

"How much did that worthless old coot get you for?"

Mittens didn't answer; his mind was miles away — floating above the rocks and pines that lined the shore of Arrow Lake, soaring over the hills and valleys near the banks of the Isabella River — looking for a lost trapper.

"Well...um...ah, I guess we'll be leaving," said the guide as he turned and motioned to his group to follow.

As they walked away, Mittens remained motionless — his mind still in a trance. When the group was a hundred feet away, he snapped to his senses and yelled, "Hey!"

As the guide turned, Mittens yelled, "Worthless? Worthless? Is a mans worth measured in dollars or in the effort spent on his rescue? Is his value on earth equal to one plane ride?"

With a puzzled look on his face, the guide mumbled to his group, "Let's get out of here. That guy has been in the woods too long."

The End